The Flowers of Autumn

A Novel and Three Short Stories

By Stephen J. Pitzen

Stephen Pitzen

The Flowers of Autumn

and the following short stories

Paradise Endured, Paradise Denied, and Snapshots

November

Magic Wands

Published by ECO Arts Publishing
PO Box 27 Benedict MN 56436
Spring 2008

Cover Photo by Don Moen Photography
Walker Minnesota

Printed in the United States of America
By Arrow Printing Bemidji Minnesota

The Flowers of Autumn was written and rewritten many times between 1982 and 2007, it is a work of fiction, the names, characters, and situations are completely imaginary. Any resemblance to actual events, or to persons living or dead is coincidental. That said the characters of Ray, Leo, and Aunty Ellen reflect the essence of people I know and have known.

I would like to thank my wife Mary whose support throughout, and typing in the early stages of writing, kept this book alive.

I also thank my father Michael F Pitzen 1917 - 1993 for taking the time to read to his children and having the patience it took to have them read to him. That was the greatest gift possible.

THE FLOWER'S OF AUTUMN

A pair of dogs running shoulder to shoulder charge down the railroad tracks apparent escapees from a group of houses to the northwest. The tracks lead to Canada, or cities far to the south, depending on which direction the freight train first sounds its warning whistle from as it enters town. Elevated above a swamp and meandering creek by a high, grass and brush covered earthen bank, the tops of the rails glisten in the sun. One dog drags a short length of chain that bounces off the ground and causes the dog to stumble slightly when he steps on it. The other is loose and free. Tongues hanging down from the grinning corners of their mouths they pause and then rush over the bank's steep edge. The lead dog is spotted but mostly brown, with something suggestive of Springer Spaniel in its ears and the wild gleam of its eyes. The snapped off piece of chain doesn't seem to interfere with his desire for adventure. It jingles as he runs. His free running companion is a stocky Labrador with a thick never still tail. They slow down and seemingly grow serious, stalking and pouncing on unseen prey. The closer they get to a slow moving stream the more cautious and purposeful their movements become. Suddenly the Labrador catches scent of something and rushes into a thick stand of cattails. The spaniel hesitates before plunging in but gets excited by his partners splashing and joins the wet pursuit. From the opposite side of the tall weeds there comes a sound of something sliding into the creeks lily pad covered back water. A small moving V appears on the water and the head of a muskrat breaks surface as it swims quietly across the shallow pond. The dogs, wet and dirty emerge from the cattails sniffing and panting just as the rodent dives and disappears beneath the bank on the other shore of the slough. Both dogs circle happily nosing the cold wet bog for some trace of their vanished quarry but gradually lose interest they move towards drier ground.

"Charlie, Charlie, you son of uh bitch. Come here!" The command came from quite a distance, but the Labrador dutifully turns and runs in the direction of the voice. The spaniel watches his friend leave and then reluctantly follows, his chain jangling as he climbs the steep bank.

The sound of pursuit having subsided, the muskrat crawls to the edge of his small den in the bank, swims down and then up to the surface of his pond. Not trusting his beady little black eyes, he pauses for several seconds and tests the air currents for danger. His nose satisfied he resumes his autumn foraging.

Overhead the sun lies low in the sky, and with every day it sinks further towards the horizon. The days grow short, the nights long and cold, plants respond to the change by dying back. The tough swamp grass alone is green and receptive absorbing low waves of energy that seem warm in this protected spot. The recent lush summer vegetation has already begun to disintegrate becoming mud where seeds seek life. Snow, frost, and rain will break down even the stems to join the leaves in a healthy rot that in a sweeping circle returns everything to fodder.

The lower torso and legs of a man stretch down the sun soaked railroad bank, sounds of snoring echo amongst the purple thistle and milkweed. A bluebottle fly warmed by the sun and brought back to life enters the copse of drying plants. The insects droning stops as it crawls across the nose of a man, awakened he makes a sluggish pass with his arm and the fly drones again as it buzzes off in the cool autumn air. His upper body appears, yawning and stretching he rises from the tall brown grass and dead weeds that had concealed him. He stands up gathering his thoughts, squinting at the sun, attempting to remember the time and place. He is a tall, heavy bodied man dressed in wrinkled clothes and a thick woolen jacket. His pants are soiled from resting when and where he grew tired. He spits the sleep from his mouth, sits back down on the bank and shakes a Camel out of a crumpled cigarette package and lights the already partially smoked cigarette. Still stretching a bit from his nap in the grass, he overlooks his world. To his left is a large white stucco structure in good repair and the brick First National Bank looking oddly out of place sandwiched between two decrepit wooden buildings. He reaches down and adjusts his underwear, breaking the strangle hold the garment had on his testicles, takes a final drag on his cigarette and stubs it out in the dirt. Below the place he sits the small creek winds its way through a cattail slough. Where the ground is slightly higher large spruce and willows have found root space and hang over the stream giving shade to its mossy bottom. This is where the pickerel hide in the spring when they spawn and children go to sit and smoke, talking, and keeping cool from the summer heat in the shadows where it's always cool and no one can see.

Grabbing the weeds, he eases his way down the steep grade. Standing among the shorter willows he sends a stream of urine into the dark peat moss and scratches the top of his head. Blackbirds sitting high on the cattail stems sing excitedly thankful for one more day spared from coming winter, another day from the long migration south. These late autumn days are full of anticipation, full of things to prepare, people putting on storm windows and cutting wood, migratory birds fattening up, muskrats storing precious roots and bulbs for winter food, everything preparing in its own way for the cold to come, either by fleeing or by some degree of hibernation.

A light north wind drifting over the cool blue water of the nearby lake chills the air. The village stretches out along a rock strewn shore. Prehistoric glacial ridges offer terraces to segregate the neighborhoods, rich from poor, old from young. The town's livelihood depends on these waters drawing weekend fishermen and vacationing families to resorts and lake homes. The travelers come to get in touch with a more natural unplanned world away from the tar and concrete, away from the landscaped cities to the south where everything is measured and assessed. The tourists are mostly gone now and the lake prepares for an ice shrouded rest, free of oily boat motors and drunks peeing into its once pure water.

The man climbs back up the railroad fill and walks towards town. His scuffed and weathered work boots make a slight slapping noise as the loose sole of the right one flip flops in cadence to his steps. His name was Carl, but for years all he has known for a name is Stump. The name for the portion of the tree men could find no use for, a thing to be sworn at, an obstacle to progress, something that always seemed to be in the way. The people who surrounded him could only see the things he wasn't.

That he couldn't measure up to the marks someone, sometime, had left for them. So he was a stump. Always there as a reminder of a deeply rooted flaw in their own body chemistry.

His pubic assistance money and Social Security check were handled by a social worker who liked Stump but had many other duties. This gave Stump a good deal of freedom and as long as he remained relatively inoffensive to public mores he could go where, and do what he pleased within the small town and surrounding countryside. His spending money was closely controlled to protect him from the people who would borrow or bully him for whatever they could get to drink on. He could eat his meals at either of two greasy cafes or at the equally greasy but much friendlier VFW club, he generally chose the latter. Every aspect of his life was open to investigation and conversation. He didn't have the cunning to conceal the things normal society knew to keep secret. He openly picked his nose and scratched his bottom. He felt things totally, his emotions, his astonishment were complete and honest. This made him a target for pranks. The butt of jokes to some, or object of misguided sympathy and unwelcome attentions from others. They would assuage their consciences by meaningless amenities on the streets and parcels of food and candy around the holidays. Either of these attentions embarrassed Stump and set him more aside, giving him less of the anonymity he craved. He thanked them for their gifts, pretended not to understand the cruelties he recognized and luckily missed the cruelest of their barbs, somehow he managed to persevere in a world full of observing eyes.

Stump would make his daily pilgrimage from whatever spot he chose for a nap to the VFW or one of the cafes and eat a burger and a bowl of soup. His diet was standard even if he had wanted something else he would have gotten the same. The waitress would see Stump walk in the door and yell, "throw a burger on for Stump". This avoided the long wait while he pretended to read the special board and ordered a hamburger anyway and it fit within the budget allowed by the welfare people. If he went to the VFW he usually had several beers with his meal and the barmaid or cook would joke with him if they weren't too busy.

Several winters before in February he'd gone into the municipal bar and a couple young men feeling the length and boredom of that month in Minnesota decided to pass the day buying "good old Stump" beers and seeing just how drunk they could get him. They kept ordering him beers and since they were paying for them the bartenders didn't feel inclined to dissuade business on an otherwise slow day, in an even slower month. One of his drinking "buddies" finally grew tired of that game and added a new dimension to something that was growing old and expensive.

"Hey Stump" he whispered, "Nancy's givin yuh the eye." Stump had ducked his head. Even in the fog of all the beer he was embarrassed and felt the need to be somewhere else. "No! No shit I think she likes yuh. Look at those tits. Uh women look at me that way, smilin I know what I'd do, youbetcha I would".

Nancy, the barmaid in question, not knowing what was being discussed, was in fact smiling in the general direction of Stump and the group that now surrounded him. What she was grinning at was a note printed on a bar napkin one of Stump's

7

companions was attempting to tape on Stump's back, "21BEERS AN STIL UPRITE". "The dumb bastards can't even spell" was the thought that made her smile.

Stump did look up then, and her smile and the beer got him to his feet, and sent him staggering towards her. His hand had barely touched her shoulder when his drinking partners descended on him in an attempt to abort the prank that was getting beyond the simple boring day diversion they had been looking for. Stump not understanding why they were grabbing him fought back. Eventually the police had to be called and by then Stump was so frightened, confused and the story concocted by the others to hide their guilt so plausible, that the officer placed Stump on a 72 hour hold and sent him to the state hospital as a threat to his own safety and the safety of others.

The memory of the arrest, the humiliation, the ride in a police car while handcuffed were memories that Stump would never lose. After several weeks of evaluation by psychiatrists in the treatment center and the snooping by his social worker, Stump was allowed to come home, with an agreement by the tavern owners that he was limited to four beers a day. By switching bars during the day he sometimes could have a few more but he was watched and never allowed to drink enough that he couldn't be controlled.

Some of the men in the bars would joke about Nancy's boyfriend whenever Stump came in. It was painful for several weeks but with time and unfortunate occurrences in other peoples lives to be brought out in the open and dissected in the public interest, Stump's humiliation was soon forgotten by the town, but not by Stump who lived in fear of what he had learned through this encounter of society's ultimate power over him.

The loose sole of his boot, the noise it made flopping up and down, reminded him of the sound his shoes had made for the first few days of his "treatment", when they had taken his shoelaces away as a suicide precaution. He decided that after eating he might go see Mr. Botts the shoemaker and have his boots fixed. The matted yellow tail of a cat sticking out of the weeds drew Stump's attention. Its head had been crushed by the Northern Pacific freight train that came through twice each day. He squatted down, thighs resting on calves and weight balanced on the balls of his feet. The cat lay mostly concealed in the tall dead grass beside the railroad tracks. It was a wild tabby tom which refused to be caught and petted. Stump had seen it many times hunting birds and had thrown rocks at him to disrupt his sneaking. Stump picked the cat up by its hind feet and tossed it underhand out into the swamp. In a slow twisting arc it fell the twenty feet and thudded down on the soft ground where it had killed so often.

He slid back down the bank and walked over to a large cement culvert that allowed the creek to flow under the tracks and earthen fill. The water here was quick. With a sandy bottom fewer weeds grew and those that did all pointed down stream with the current. They snapped and whipped out a dance of life that kept time to the songs of birds and the pulse of the seasons. Wild and full of abandon with the springs melting snow, slower and rhythmic in a summer drought, the tempo was fast today with the runoff of the seasonal rains. The water was cold and clear. So clear you could read the label on an algae encrusted Nesbitt's bottle in mid stream. Stump used a long stick to rake the beverage container in to where he could reach it. Plunging his hands into the water he retrieved the bottle and then washed the slime off it and the smell of feline death off his hands. He slid the bottle into the deep coat pocket and wiped his hands off on his pants leg.

He waited there sitting on the culvert's lip and listened for the noon whistle from the fire station to call him to lunch. A large moss backed snapping turtle passed under him and through the culvert traveling downstream toward the lake and its winter sleep on the silty bottom. A flock of swans flew over as he waited. Their long necks thrust out, bodies making serpentine dips and rises to the steady beat of massive wings they called sadly and quietly as they passed above.

Stump witnessed all of these changes and could feel similar powers working on his body and emotions, a melancholy short of true depression that left him more taciturn than normal and tired even after a good nap. Most people felt the same shift but didn't have or take the time to watch the world shutting down around them, so they drank more and talked less. They grew surly and felt like staying in bed and not going to work. Their chemical ties to nature kept mind in constant battle with spirit and season. Small wonder that they resented Stump and anyone else that took, or had the time, to watch the seasons change and time stand still. They were seen as dregs on society neither producing nor consuming enough to benefit anyone. They kept social workers working and bleeding hearts soothed. All at the expense of those who were too busy to sit on culverts and watch the flight of swans. They didn't have the luxury of taking time. It was their only commodity, to be used for bettering oneself and in most cases for simple survival of themselves and their families.

With the piercing shriek of the noon whistle Stump left the creek. Taking a short cut across the weed spotted skating rink and up a short hill past the rear entrance to the fire station. Emma Schwartz nodded at him as he passed her window in city hall which took up most of the top floor of the combined fire, police and town government building that still proudly proclaimed that it had been built by the WPA. He waved back timidly knowing that much of what affected his life and freedom was controlled by what was seen and heard by the lady who had just acknowledged his existence.

As he walked passed the Philco Radio and TV Repair he paused to look in the window. Televisions with their backs removed, tubes glowing in some, sat in dusty rows waiting for a part or a payment to release them from limbo. Stump peered at the glass and examined his reflection. He brushed the dead grass out of his hair and off the shoulders and back of his coat and pants. His face seemed cleaner than on some days. His mother would have scrubbed him thoroughly and given his ears a much needed scrounging but she was dead as was his father. In their place his social worker stopped by every week to check out his room at the Lakeshore and drop well intended hints and occasional ultimatums in regards to Stump's hygiene. So at least once a week he was forced to shave, bathe and put on the cleanest clothes that he could find in his closet. These he would wear until the next meeting, and when he started digging out things his caseworker had already rejected on previous visits, Stump would be directed to the laundromat. Stump felt himself lucky and it a minor victory when occasionally his worker was feeling benevolent or apathetic enough to pass on clothes that had failed muster before.

Stump's parents were both fairly old when he was born and were dead by the time he had reached twenty three. They had stopped sending him to school when he was in the third grade. That was when the school suggested that he would do better at the State School in Brainerd where they were more equipped to deal with his needs. They could have said he would be better off with his own kind and it would have meant the same to Stump's mother. She politely refused their suggestion.

The school reported the problem to the Welfare Department and his mother told the county worker to get off her property the next time the proposal was made. Both agencies considered their duty done and promptly forgot about Stump and left his education to whatever his parents could provide to him. They tried to teach him to read, but never could, and he learned his limited math and money skills by buying things on the Saturday trips to town. More importantly his parents demonstrated to him by their actions how to get along with each other and the world they lived in. Social skills that would keep him out of the state institutions where "his kind" were sent to vegetate, away from the threads of nature, society, and culture that could keep them from becoming even less acceptable to the community that had produced them, and away from the only environment where those skills could be learned. Stump led a sheltered life on a brush forty farm west of town until his father died. At that time his mother moved into town, sold the farm, and moved into the Lakeshore Hotel. She survived her husband by several years and in that time Stump learned about town life, where to pee without getting in trouble, and to look before stepping out into the street. His mother in her last years acted as a buffer between Stump and the consequences of his offending townspeople with behaviors that were just part of the day to day of life in the middle of nowhere. By the time she passed on Stump was a part of the town and had acquired the social repertoire needed to stay out of serious trouble. Stump finished his inspection and walked the few remaining steps to his destination.

Deep fats welcome mat drew him in. The VFW's grill and French fry cooker were fired up and serving the lunchtime crowd. Leo the bartender looked up seeing Stump he turned to the cook, "Throw one on for Stump,"

The cook a timeless woman who could have been any age over sixty fired back, "I'm not blind yuh know, I saw him comin half uh block away for Chrisesake."

Leo shrugged good-naturedly and the cook grabbed a thick slab of ground meat and dropped it down on the already sizzling griddle where four other burgers and a mound of sliced onions were frying and filling the small barroom with their rich pungent odor. Leo was a big man with a white apron tied high around his thick waist. The apron had spots of hamburger grease and the red sauce of the chili that constantly simmered in a twenty quart soup kettle at the back of the grill.

Stump felt most comfortable here. The customers were more honest; working men and women who chose to ignore him, or to talk if they had something to say. At

10

some of the cafes people seemed to feel duty bound to mouth a few things usually telling him the time of day, "Morning," "Afternoon". Some of the more jovial or talkative ones would update him on their opinion of the daily weather. This attention only made Stump feel uncomfortable and more conspicuous. He would eat his breakfasts and an occasional supper other places but the VFW was where he spent most of his lunch times and rainy days. When the weather was serious outside he would slowly suck on a mug of beer and sit out the day watching the unemployed or rained out workers shake dice, play cards and drink beer. He would quietly join in their laughter or remain silent and concentrate if the game grew serious. In small ways such as this he remained a member of the community.

The daily movements of Stump though constant and fairly predictable were monitored. Daily tabs kept. If he altered his schedule, note was taken and questions asked. The watching of Stump became a part of daily life and a topic of conversation over more dinner tables than Stump could have imagined. By evening the simple throwing of a dead cat over a cliff could become, "Yuh know yuh can't trust that Stump around cats", to a theory that he had a pattern of cat mutilation. Depending on the day, the month, or the boredom, these stories were either disparaged or likely to bring up the assertion that something would eventually have to be done about him or he would end up hurting someone. He was a diversion as necessary to the survival of the small town as the appearance of Mayor Nelson at the long table in the "Outdoorsman" each morning.

Without the relatively harmless pastime of "Stump watching", more time would have been available to examine the lives of people less vulnerable but more easily hurt by the insatiable appetites of the gossip hungry. Stump wasn't aware of much of the interest shown in him. When he did feel himself the object of someone's scrutiny he usually became nervous and started digging in his nose or ears and generally they would find something else to look at. Several years ago he had noticed that when he would come in at night his neighbor's door would quietly shut when he came up the stairs from the lobby below. It was winter and as much as he craved sleep during those torturous long nights he also liked to keep his own hours and not feel that he didn't have any privacy. He started taking long walks and looking at the immense cold sky and the endless display of stars that shed so little light. Hands stuffed deep in pockets filled with some mostly clean napkins, some useless hard paper wads with no useful nose wipes left in them, and empty Camel packs, he walked and waited for Mrs. Berg to give up her wait and go to bed. After several days she was telling her morning coffee group that they better start keeping their drapes drawn shut because "Stump is keeping some perty unusual hours", and she didn't think any good could be coming from that. The nightly wanderings continued until the bitter cold would drive Stump into the VFW or Municipal Liquor Store where he would wait for closing time. A month later the battle ended with Stump so tired from his nocturnal prowling that he gave up and willing to accept the spying, and Mrs. Berg too worn down from staying awake late at night and walking down the cold hallway to peer out the window at the deserted street below to maintain her vigilance.

Stump surveyed the crowded bar and walked back to a worn formica table with even more tattered booth seats. Leo was talking to a group of out of town hunters as he fixed plates for the burgers and tended the bar.

"What you fellers huntin for?"

The oldest of the group stopped in mid rattle of the dice cup. "We're just tryin to get our deer stands put up before the snow starts fallin. If we stumble across uh duck dumb enough to fly into range he'd be in trouble but he better come damn close to uh bar stool. When's the action pick up around here?"

"Bout June or July if it's uh cold spring."

A younger member of the group laughed a little longer than really necessary as was appropriate for an out of towner asking a sensitive question. "No we're serious, any stray stuff ever come in here?"

Leo slid two burger plates and accompanying beers across the bar to a pair of cement stained construction workers. He reached down and wiped his fingers on the underside of his apron, "might be later on some girls will be round the Muney or one of the other bars. Course all the summer gals are gone so it won't pay to get choosy."

Ellen the cook snorted in contempt of the choosy statement, "Since when's any body that's got to ask where the girls are been choosy." she accented choosy by pushing sharply down on a well browned paddy and making it sizzle on the hot grill.

Leo grinned at the hunters, "Yuh been gettin any ducks."

"Oh uh few, the weathers been too damn nice, there all settin out in the middle eatin rice."

Leo looked up and down the bar and said in a lower voice, "You fellers wouldn't want to take uh few fish home with yuh would'ja."

The older man once again answered. "Sure should have sumpthin to show the women except for red eyes, empty wallets and sore dicks." His group laughed and the cook snorted her derision for the comment.

Leo again scanned the room. "I can't get yuh nothin, but I know uh couple fellas that could get yuh some walleyes an as many whitefish as yuh want. Can't say for sure cuz I don't have nothin to do with it, but they might be willin to help yuh out."

"How much money yuh talkin about?"

Leo scratched his stubble covered chin and glanced around the room. "Buck uh piece for whitefish and three for walleyes."

"Seems kind uh high for uh stinkin damn whitefish but I'll take uh half dozen of them walleyes if there's any size to em." The older man's friends all nodded in agreement to his order.

"Hey Stump come get your lunch, I ain't got the help to cart it out to yuh."

Stump walked to the end of the bar where Leo had carried his plate.

"When yuh get done with that if yuh can find Sam Cloud I'll buy yuh uh beer if yuh tell him to stop by before dark." Leo was whispering so Stump nodded his head in silent agreement. He finished his message to Stump and turned back to the hunters.

"Can't make any guaranty but stop back here bout ten tonight and there might be uh feller that could help yuh out." As Leo walked by the beer tap he poured a mug of Schmidt's and gave it a back handed slide down the bar to his companion in crime. Stump grinned, ignorant of his involvement in a game violation and sipped his beer knowing that it wouldn't count against his daily limit.

Leo wiped the drip pan under the beer tap and looked warily at the older hunter. "Yuh pay me an don't give this feller any crap about how much he wants for his fish or yuh might end up with uh whitefish enema." The hunters laughed, ordered another pitcher of beer, two moved to the pool table in the back of the tavern and looked it over.

Stump joined in the laughter, after his tour in the state hospital he had more than a passing acquaintance with enemas and he had helped Sam with his nets enough that he was quite familiar with the size and shape of whitefish but the picture of the one being done with the other was difficult to imagine. He decided to save it for Sam later and see if he could decipher it.

Leo turned to the cement spattered construction workers, "What you fellers up to?"

"Lissnin to you break the law, yuh old fart don't yuh know any better then to sell fish to tourists."

"I ain't sold jack shit! Just so happens I know uh feller that might be able to help them fellers out. It's like I'm makin their trip up north more enjoyable. Doin uh public service yuh might say. Like the chamber uh commerce only better cuz I'm helpin out the poor and down trodden."

"Bull shit Leo! Sam Cloud never has charged more then two bucks for uh walleye."

"What are yuh some kind uh communist, every bodies gotta make uh livin."

"I'll be sure to tell Hoger that, he's awful understandin bout that sort'a thing, and I know damn well he ain't uh communist."

Leo laughed deeply, "Shit Glen if yuh told Hoger he'd just figger you was just tryin to get him off yer tail so yuh could poach uh venison."

"I ain't violated in two years. Been legal ever since I got caught with the live one in my trunk."

One of the hunters looked at the man Leo had called Glen. "How'd yuh end up with uh live deer in yer trunk?"

Glen smiled reflectively and sipped his beer. "Bout two years ago we was workin over on the Range, damn good job too till the good ore started to peter out, anyway we was comin home from Chisholm one night, not plannin nothin illegal, just drivin home for the weekend and sippin uh few with Bud here."

Bud nodded his head in always ready support of that statement or anything truthful or otherwise that Glen might say.

"Well anyway we were on 200 bout three miles this side of Remer when this dandy doe steps out of the ditch and freezes just as perty as yuh please. I was drivin the old Dodge and goin kind uh slow since we was drinkin so I got stopped bout twenty feet from it. I had the 45 under the seat so's I pull it out. She's still standin there like uh dumb shit lookin at the headlights." Glen looked sadly at his nearly empty beer mug and shook the last quarter of an inch around, quietly staring in disbelief at his bad fortune.

The pause grew into an interlude. Finally one of the hunters perceived the signal, "Could we get yuh uh round there," Glen and Bud nodded reluctantly, "Leo could yuh set those guys up with two more."

Leo collected the mugs and poured two frothy headed drinks for the story teller and his faithful companion. Glen used his somewhat dirty forefinger to scrape off the suds and gave Leo a look of silent disapproval. Leo smiled but otherwise ignored the critique.

"Well thanks fellers damn nice of yuh. Like I was sayin this deer just stood there, so I rolled down the window and poked the 45 out. I rested the barrel there on the door edge." He paused and took a long drink of the pale amber liquid and sighed appreciatively. "Well I aims right for the head figgerin that at this distance ain't no way I'm gonna miss." Glen padded his shirt pockets as if searching for something. The older hunter who had ordered the beer sensed the need and reached into his own pocket and extended a pack of cigarettes towards Glen. "No offense but I can't smoke Kool's somethin bout menthol gags me, anybody gotta Camel." Stump got up and brought Glen a cigarette more to his liking. "Thanks much Stump". He tamped the end on the wooden bar top and accepted the light from the ever ready Bud. "Where was I? Oh yea, I pulled the trigger and inside that damn car it sounded like a cannon went off. I think we was both bout half deaf for uh week after that. Well that doe went down and I mean she didn't even wiggle. Then all of uh sudden Bud here spots headlights bout uh mile or so back toppin uh hill." Bud nodded his head in agreement and smiled basking in the attention his part of the drama drew to him. "Anyways I jumps out and screw around tryin to find the right key in the dark and then tryin to find the damn hole, all the time this damn cars gettin closer to us, Bud runs over and grabs the deer by the legs and skids it back quick to the car and by then I finally got the trunk open. It was uh big doe must uh weighed close to 200 pounds with its guts in and we sure as hell didn't have time to be guttin it out with that car barreling down on us so we tossed it in the trunk and got the hell out uh there quick. Shit we was only hundred yards down the road before we met the car and damned if it wasn't uh highway patrol."

Stump eased to the edge of the booths bench seat. He'd heard this story a number of times but Glen was a good storyteller and he seemed to remember it differently or add to it, so it grew more entertaining with each telling.

"So we decided it best to put uh few miles between us and the scene of the crime, but then we started to get thirsty and we pulled in for uh quick one at the Swede's out at the junction. We figured that would give some time for things to cool down. I think I was on my second beer when this young pup of uh deputy comes runnin in yellin bout someone bein locked in the trunk of a 59 Dodge and how they was kickin the hell out of it tryin to escape. The whole bar ran out into the parking lot and sure enough the most godawfull hammerin and bawlin was comin out of the trunk uh that car. Big ole dents and buckles in the sheet metal and yuh know that old Dodge was made out uh good steel not like this crap today. Anyway the deputy yells, whose car is this, and the Swede recognizes it and puts the finger on me. I opens up the trunk and out jumps the deer and it's off runnin before its feet even touch ground. Must uh just bounced that bullet off its head, hardly bled in the trunk at all." Glen took his final swallow of beer, set the mug down, and looked at Bud as if the unavoidable time to go back to work had arrived.

"Did yuh get uh fine or anything."

"Nea they had such uh good laugh over it they just warned me, and what the hell, the evidence ran off, all they could a got me for was kidnapping uh deer. I'll bet that deer is still runnin."

The hunters shook their heads in amazement and ordered another pitcher of beer and two more mugs for Glen and Bud, who seemed relieved to put off their return to work.

Four more men walked in and took the remaining bar stools. They were younger than Glen and his companion but also had cement spattered clothes on. They stood straighter and didn't have the look of resignation on their faces or in their posture that was as much a part of the older two as the scuffed and oily Chippewa boots on their feet or the faded dusty caps perched on the back of their heads, but they were young and with years and injuries they too would walk in stooped and look for excuses to stay long, anything was preferable to pouring cement and lifting concrete blocks.

Leo poured them a pitcher without asking. They ordered burgers and chili, asked for the dice box and started shaking to see who would pay for the beer. One of the men looked at the cook and asked, "Hey Aunty Ellen yuh gettin any?" His friends and most in the bar laughed.

Ellen looked over the top of her glasses at the much younger man, "Just enough to keep the hole open." The entire bar laughed at her come back especially the one who had opened the topic for discussion. "And if either of my sisters would uh had uh kid as ugly as you they'd of taught him some manners cause cute you ain't."

Stump wiped his plate clean with a small piece of hamburger bun and left the bar quietly. As he reached the door Leo called out to him, "Remember to tell Sam to stop in if yuh see him."

Stump knew it was pointless to look for Sam this early in the day, later, down by the boat landing he would talk to him, when he came in from checking net. Stump walked up the street and turned into the entryway of the Lakeshore Hotel. In the lobby two of the old timers that kept rooms in the hotel were watching "Days of Our Lives" and the owner gave Stump a wave as he passed through on his way to the steps. Stump walked up three flights of stairs to the top floor and down the hall to his room. After standing the soda bottle against the wall with a dozen others, he lay down on the bed, folded his hands behind his head, and stared up at the ceiling. He remembered entire days in the state hospital lying like this. Some people on his ward had spent their entire adult life and much of their childhood in a drug imposed stupor, malleable but decomposing, staring at nothing, in beds they seldom left. His ceiling was at least interesting, there were elephants on the tiles, continents and islands never charted by explorers. Their brown masses expanding with each rain, encompassing the neighboring tiles like conquerors or locusts, like the spread of a plague going out in all directions. Dark shapes that changed not only with time and moisture but becoming what the observer looked for, sometimes subservient to mood, wish and thought, sometimes capable of controlling them. Today they were faces, old weary men looking sadly down on him with eyes bereft of any compassion but sorrowful none the less. Stump shifted to his side not wanting to look at them any more but knowing too well that once the stains assumed a shape in his mind it took a long time for them to change to something else. Sighing deeply he bunched up his pillow and stared at the closet door. Two months after being released from the institution Stump had found a single shot shotgun tossed in the weeds north of town. Lying in the ditch where its previous owner had thrown it after a screwed up robbery, sawed off barrel and stock filthy, he wrapped it neatly into his coat and concealed it there on the walk home. The gun now lay hidden behind a boot box in the hardest to get at corner of the closet. Even his social worker on his most thorough shakedown had feigned the inspection of that dark corner, so it had lain gathering dust, but the central part of Stump's only plan of defense against a system he now feared.

The worker was supposed to come by today and do his weekly visit. Stump looked forward to these meetings, sometimes they would go for coffee, but often they would just talk. The man was young and still fresh enough from school to be challenged by the huge caseload, not yet hardened to his job and the routine of dealing with people being beaten to death one disappointment at a time by reality. Once at the State Hospital he had asked Stump if he needed anything, Stump had said crackers and sardines would be nice. The next visit he brought the treats and sat with him to make sure he was allowed to eat them. The worker had set him free, the doctors, police, and lawyers would have left him there to rot after deciding it was what was in his best interest, and it was the worker that made it possible for him to stay out of state care. He waited for his knock and company but still kept the weapon hidden.

Chapter 2

At 3:45 three children balancing precariously on a ribbon of steel walked in slow deliberation placing one foot in front of the other on their smooth, solid tightrope. On their left lay the swamp the man Stump had spent the late morning napping beside. The autumn sun was far to the west now and shadows from nearby pines and spruce covered the area in cool darkness. The children peered over the steep embankment hoping to see him in his sleeping place.

"What do yuh think he does down there Philip?" The smallest of the three asked this as he hopped off the rail and sat on the end of a creosote blackened tie.

"He just sleeps mostly, but I heard he hides stuff he swipes in those weeds." Philip said this in an ominous tone and with a look of somehow secret knowledge on his thin, large eared face.

All three looked down again at the spot. Curiosity and caution competed, Anne the oldest and more assertive threw a test rock into the thicket of milkweed and scrub willow. When no response came to their inquiry they started the climb down the bank. Up in front of the Lakeshore a loud lawn mower like noise and a backfire made them stop and look past City Hall. A light blue Corvaire backed out of a parking spot and roared down the street. The children recognized it as the county worker's car and as they stared Stump stepped out of the hotel and walked away from them and towards downtown. Feeling braver they slid giggling down hill into the copse of weeds.

They examined the area of matted grass where the weight of a body had left a telltale impression. There was a bare spot on the ground that seemed promising but all it produced was a handful of crushed out cigarette butts and a collection of various candy bar wrappers. Tim prodded around in the taller grass at the edges of the laying spot with the toe of his shoe. He squatted down and peered under the willows.

Philip joined in the search. "I don't see no blood round here. If he tortured animals there'd be lots of it, and hair too. I heard Deak Johnson tellin everybody he'd seen Stump killin stuff down here lots uh times."

"He must uh been lyin. My sister says he makes up lots uh stories." Anne's tone put an end to speculations about animal mutilations.

She was the first to reach the swamp's edge. There was a makeshift bridge across the wettest part of the slough. Made of old and discarded tires, planks, logs and high hummocks of swamp grass, it was treacherous even when all caution was used in navigating the crossing. A step to either side would drop the traveler in the soupy loon crap that everyone claimed made up the underworld below a cattail bog. Anne made the passage safely. Tim was nearly across when Philip tried to splash the other two by jumping on the end of a plank and getting the boards bouncing to create a spray of mud for the other two's amusement and discomfort. As luck would have it his feet slipped on the sodden wood and he fell backwards into the sloppy mixture of water and partially rotted cattail stalks. Tim had a few spots sprayed on his pants legs and Anne was missed entirely by the flying debris. Philip crawled out of the muck his labored steps making suctioning plops as he struggled to free himself from the cold wet mud that oozed around his skinny waist. Between bouts of laughter Anne and Tim safe on the willow limbs offered encouragement and helpful suggestions which Philip responded to with the extent of his limited profanity.

The swamp was a slow gentle place of water held back by generation after generation of gradually deposited silt and the vegetation that took root there. In spite of it's harmlessness it was still off limits to the children and that made it all the more irresistible. Their mothers saw it as a dirty place full of laundry hazards and too much freedom. In Philip's home getting caught in the swamp or with the muddy evidence of having been there on your clothes meant at least a grounding, and a thorough dousing such as this could mean the switch. He crawled out on the bank and looked down at his soiled school clothes. In the summer he would have washed them out in the creek, hung them from a willow branch and waited out the drying period in his underwear. All three had spent long warm summer days with play clothes hanging in the wind counting on time and evaporation to erase their crime.

A cool evening breeze from the lake flowed over the railroad bank and stirred through the cattails. Philip was sitting on the willow's trunk where it lay down over the stream and touched water. His lower legs were dangling down in the creek and causing the current to push water up over his lap. With his hands he scooped even more up and scrubbed vigorously at the mud soaked blue school pants. As he sat he kicked his legs up and down. The muck from his trousers washed slowly off in the stream. Drifting down it settled to the bottom of backwater holes where the children hunted tadpoles in the late spring.

He looked up from his washing, "What yuh wanna do tomorrow?"

Anne who was climbing on a higher limb answered, "Were gonna go to Bermidgi an see are Ant Lisa cuz she had uh baby."

"Was it uh boy or uh girl?"

"I don't know Ma said they called it Shawn or maybe Shauna, it's too little to play with so it don't matter much."

Tim pulled a dried jewel weed stalk out of the soft marshy ground and threw it and the attached root ball into the creek. "Where did Ant Lisa get her baby?"

Philip looked up knowingly, "Deak Johnson told me that uh man pees where uh woman pees and then she gets uh baby."

"In the toilet?" Tim's face was even more incredulous than his voice.

"No! Not in the toilet! Yuh know down there." Philip pointed in the general direction of "down there" on his body to illustrate more clearly his claim.

"Deak is full uh shit, my ma says him an that whole bunch he hangs with are gonna end up in jail and that their so stupid that's the best place for em."

Philip looked up, "No really my brother Fred said he was tellin the truth."

Anne looked both boys over with contempt, "I said he's full uh shit and I meant it. You boys are so stupid! I gotta book that'll show yuh the whole thing but yer too young to see it now."

Philip who was coldest led crossing the swamp and over the bank. As they

18

hurried down the railroad tracks he asked, "Anne can I go to yer house an throw my stuff in yer dryer?"

"No my ma worked the 3:30 today, she'd catch us all, an if you get caught don't squeal on us."

At an intersection of tracks and street Anne split off with her younger brother in tow. They walked across the street and into a small yellow house, "yellow like uh dead canary's ass," that's what Phillip's father had to say about not only the color choice but the general upkeep of the Petersen house. They did have an automatic clothes dryer and Philip right at that moment would have traded a whole block of perfectly painted homes for 15 minutes with his trousers and underwear rolling around in the super heated bowels of the electric marvel. Philip headed up a slight hill and turned left on Lake Street.

The Anderman's had moved into town when Philip was three years old. His father had tried to make a living on the land his father had farmed, but soil and climate resisted his every effort. The acres of land he cleared had stumps to fight. Rocks heaved up by each frost jarred his teeth and dulled the plow. The cows had a greater chance of getting a stone bruised heel than a full stomach in his pastures. Thousands of boulders, some the size of his tractor, all climbing each year inch by inch out of the confining earth. Smaller rocks were hauled away on a stone boat. The larger ones grew where they wanted, a source of constant irritation to every phase of the farming year. It was as if the earth had cursed him, rewarding his labor with feldspar and gneiss, instead of oats or barley. When the banker stopped acknowledging his waves he sold the marginal farm land and planted pine on the acres that no one wanted. The irony of turning land he had stolen from Jack Pine and Poplar back into forest ate away at the insides of Mr. Anderman. He started drinking and coming home late into the night hoping that if he stayed away his family wouldn't see on him all the failure that he felt. In the spring of the third year he drove out from town to see his young pines. Candles of new growth were raised up in groups of obscenely outstretched fingers and he felt the earth was sending him a signal. He smiled and went home.

Philip didn't understand all that had happened but he was happy that his father wasn't so ornery in the morning. His mother also seemed to be easier to please and there seemed to be more laughter. He couldn't remember living on the farm, even on picnics when his brothers would show where their room had been he would say he remembered but he didn't. The farm was fun for him. He had no memories of the work it had been for his older brothers or for his father. He would have cheerfully left town life and taken up living in the slowly collapsing homestead. As he walked towards home Philip played the step on the crack game, not out loud but to himself. Sometimes he tried to avoid them and others were stomped with his still squishy black school shoes. With the same inconsistencies his mother was spared or teachers rewarded with broken backs. Most of the squares of cement still wore the WPA stamp and in the harsh climate there wasn't a shortage of cracks to leap or land on.

No one was home when Philip cautiously opened the front door. He lived in a two story house at the end of Lake Street, its paint was cracked and peeling, but a respectable white with red trim. The building was cold. What little insulation it had was lying at the bottom of the walls sent there by gravity and time. The poorly fitted windows rattled and slurped in and out in the breeze. Plastic sheeting nailed up for weather proofing sucked in and ballooned out, creating a strange rhythm that played through the seasons until spring. Despite its weathered appearance there was a sense of life here. More than just the frost nipped pots of marigolds that clung stubbornly to life or the clumsy elementary school Halloween cutouts taped on the windows. The house itself had an aura. From down the block an observer of it could have counted on the smell of good food welcoming him at the door. There was much more to this house than dry rot and missing shingles. A large portion of this atmosphere of home had left a note on the kitchen table signed Ma, and warning all readers to leave the lid on the kettle that simmered on the stove, and keep their hands off the cake that cooled near the note. Philip, seizing an opportunity to avoid being grounded, or possibly worse, headed for the basement and down its narrow runged steps. He walked back into the corner behind the furnace where the laundry hung from a crisscrossing of clotheslines. Pants, socks, underwear all wet and by now like ice on the skin were shed and warm dry replacements soon plucked from the line and drawn over bony appendages. Philip concealed the still dripping evidence on the last line nearest the furnace. The basement smelled like apples. Winesaps and Jonathans in boxes were stacked on the shelves by the wringer washer. The rusty oil furnace squatted mid floor, a huge ogre, feet spread wide and mouth-like door frowning. In the winter it grumbled and hissed as water turned to steam in its bowels. Dirty gunny sacks were lined up against the north wall. Long white strands of potato sprouts had threaded their way through the loose weave of one reaching out tentacles seeking sunlight. The other bags had fresh black soil clinging, marring the light brown burlap. Beneath the steps shelving had been attached to the risers. Rows of glass jars filled with fruit and vegetables stood ready for winter use. The cement floor was covered with sawdust, wood chips, potato dirt and the tissue wrappers from summer fruit that had been put away in jars or eaten fresh. His father's work bench was fastened to the west wall. Tools were strewn about mixed in with the odds and ends of daily life, if it didn't fit elsewhere it ended up here.

Philip placed his shoes on the soap caked tray of the deep scrub sink and slipped on a pair of scuffed black shoes without bothering to untie them. The broken back evidenced a pattern of similar use.

"Philip where you at? I see your tracks on the floor. You ain't been down at that dirty old swamp have yuh?"

"Down here Ma."

"What yuh doin in the basement."

Philip grabbed a small apple from the open box. "Just gettin somethin to eat."

He bit into the soft Jonathan and chewed off enough to verify his story.

"Well get up here and carry in some groceries."

Philip tromped up the stairs making sure each step created as much noise as his meager frame could produce. His mother was in the kitchen putting away the spoilable items in a round topped Frigidaire. Billows of smoky steam seeped out of the iced up freezer compartment in the corners where the ice jam kept its lid from closing.

"What did yuh do in school today?"

"Nothin much."

"I'm sure yuh must uh done somethin."

"We did some spelling," he ran through his day and couldn't come up with anything in particular that he'd done so he added, "and timeses we worked on them uh while too." They always seemed to spend a big chunk of every day drilling with multiplication flash cards. Philip had mastered them long ago so he daydreamed about his weekend and looked out the window. While he didn't hate school, it did interfere with his plans occasionally.

Philip's mother looked her age. Years of stretching the food budget with potatoes and macaroni, bearing five children and twenty some years of work had robbed her of the youth she hadn't taken the time to experience. She had tiny strong hands that could work all day canning vegetables in boiling hot water baths and still have enough feeling to find the spot that hurt and caress the pain away.

"What cha get to eat Ma," Philip asked as he peered around his mother into the crowded shelves of the refrigerator.

"Never mind what's in there, you just finish yer apple an wait for supper. Be uh good boy now an go get those last two bags of groceries an I'll see about makin some frosting for that cake."

This seemed to be a fair deal to Philip since he would end up carrying in the bags anyway. He walked the well beaten path out to the curb in front of the house. There had been talk about cementing it at one time, but a broken tooth and a new used car had sucked up the money, and if everyone took the same route to the street the grass couldn't grow on the hard packed dirt. He opened the rear passenger door on a long gray Chevy with large tail fins that ticked slowly as it cooled. With one bag of groceries in his arms he saw Frank walking in a detached, self conscious, cool saunter up the street towards him. Philip didn't understand Frank anymore. Frank didn't either. At sixteen he was Philip's third oldest brother. Baptized in ignorance to find forgiveness of sins he hadn't yet committed, confirmed by promises he made to lead a purer life just as he entered the utter confusion of puberty, he was a painful mixture of building passions and unbearable guilt. The natural feelings that consumed him whenever he saw anything suggestive of sex tormented him constantly because nearly everything made him think about sex. Confessing sins that were really only thoughts and doing penance longing to have committed the crime. He would kneel, pray for a while and then start thinking, wondering if he had been there long enough to satisfy his mother, noticing girls going into the confessional, eventually the cycle would begin again, prayer was a tired soldier in the battle of adolescent chemistry versus medieval morality.

"Hey Frank, why don't yuh carry the other bag in? Ma's gonna make uh dessert."

Frank had just walked Patti Richardson all the way to the curb in front of her house so he was in an exceptional mood. He grabbed the remaining bag from the back seat of the Chevy and took the bag from Philip. They walked side by side back to the house.

"Did yuh walk old ugly Patti home from school?" Philip was aware of Frank's interest in the girl and was curious to see how good his brother's mood was.

"Better keep yer twerpy mouth shut or I'll tell Ma bout three shitbirds I saw sittin in the willow down by the creek."

"Better not or I'll tell bout you sayin uh bad word." He knew better then saying the word himself and being caught in the same net.

Frank recognized a standoff and felt that was fine, everything was fine. He would have been home long before Philip but he'd dawdled in front of Patti's talking about school and the million things people find to talk about when they don't want to say goodbye. During their awkward conversation the night's football game was brought up, and yes she was planning on going, and didn't really have any plans of walking there with anyone, and it would be ok if they walked there together. It was as close to a date as Frank had ever come and he was bursting with excitement. He thought her eyes were beautiful, the color of a mountain stream in snow. They could see inside of him and that they weren't disgusted with what they saw. When she laughed at his jokes they sparkled like a sky full of stars. He had it bad. When she looked at him his heart seemed to pump so hard that it drained all of his strength for its own use. He became even more awkward and his speech became a garbled mess of partial sentences interrupted by pauses that fed on themselves while his brain panicked in search of the exact topic he'd started out talking about. To him every move she made was purposeful and fluid he couldn't imagine her experiencing similar emotions caused by his presence, but sometimes in class when he was staring at her and she would look up he felt as if a thousand thoughts would pass between them in a second and she would smile and blush.

Philip couldn't believe his ears, Frank was humming "She Loves You" and Frank always claimed to hate the Beatles. He was even smiling.

The two boys walked into the kitchen and Frank sat the bags down on the marble like formica topped table. They both grabbed handfuls of green grapes out of a bowl sitting mid-table and wandered off into the living room where they plopped down on opposite ends a faded green couch. The sofa looked as if thousands of bottoms had taken turns pounding up and down on it and like soft hammers working on an even softer anvil the cushions sagged and armrests showed bared padding through carefully placed doilies. They sat there munching grapes and playing the stare down game each waiting the other's blink or look away.

"God yer ugly, yuh can't be related to me. Ma must uh switched kids at the hospital an ended up with uh science experiment. Some kind uh baboon cross mix I'd guess."

Philip looked at his older brother and took in the scornful words without blinking keeping a serious expression on his large eared and somewhat simian looking face.

"My guess is the goverment shut em down after one look at you."

Philip slowly placed a grape in his already full mouth and allowed Frank a better view of the mastication process than he seemed prepared for. The older boy looked away in disgust Philip grinned and swallowed the pulpy cud.

Mrs. Anderman entered the room and saw them, "Why aren't yuh at work Frankie?"

Frank worked at Eikilson's Market every weekend and most nights after school. He'd asked for the night off, Mr. Eikilson, seeing Patti waiting outside, sensed a moment to be both gracious and practical on a slow afternoon, readily agreed to the time off. He knew the peaked look of longing love so well after twenty years of hiring teenagers to bag groceries that he realized Frank would be about as useful as a box of frozen lettuce. So off Frank had sailed with the first of what he hoped would be several answered prayers behind him.

"I wanted it off to get some stuff done is all."

"What sort uh stuff?" Philip inquired.

"None uh yer business, just stuff that's all." He stared with a look so full of menace that Philip remembered his vulnerability and settled back into the couch to watch his mother go to work. She was sharp eyed and studying Frank with the curiosity that made her not only a successful mother but made the lives of her children a living hell. She seized on to the smallest clue and interrogated slowly allowing no sidetracking or partial admissions. When she felt it was something she needed to, or wanted to know, she extracted the story bit by painful bit.

Frank felt an inquisition coming on and went straight to the truth. "I asked Patti if she'd go to the game with me tonight."

Philip started making a gagging noise and rolled his eyes into a crossed position. His mother quietly returned him to quiet and an upright posture with a look of un-amused disapproval.

Philip didn't really have anything against Patti, she was usually friendly or simply ignored him but it seemed to him that when his two older brothers started dating that they stopped being a close part of the family. A wall was walked through that couldn't be re-crossed and he ended up losing a brother and gained a new adult in the home.

"Patti, let's see she's the Richardson's oldest girl isn't she?" Her question was answered by a quiet nod. Mrs. Anderman felt relieved she knew the girl and the family, solid and decent, a girl that wouldn't expect a lot of money thrown at her and a family that wouldn't allow late night partying or young men hanging around interfering with their daughter's studies.

The Slayton's across the street had a daughter that gave Mrs. Anderman nightmares. Young men of all ages paraded past the house in their cars. The young and single when the sun was out, others at night when they should have been home with their wives. Doors would shut and she would be picked up or dropped off and Mrs. Anderman would wonder where her second oldest, Tom, was at.

When the ladies had coffee some would ask how much longer she could get by wearing those tight jeans and who the child might end up looking like, Mrs. Anderman prayed and remained silent.

Tom was a senior and had offers of scholarships from several state colleges to play football for them. He wasn't a bad student and had somehow avoided the trouble others with less luck had gotten into for attending the same social events that he had. Mrs. Anderman always worried that his luck would run out and that they would get a call from the sheriff or an expectant grandparent. She could see the chance of college disappear and Tom faced with the choice of a meaningless "back" job or the military. Her oldest boy John had picked the Navy when given those options. She didn't want another of her sons disappearing into a world that existed so far away from what she would ever see.

"Do yuh want the car for yer date tonight?"

"It ain't really uh date Ma! I don't know why yuh gotta make such a big deal outta this, were just goin to the game is all." Frank was turning red from the attention being paid to an area he was so unsure of.

"Okay do yuh want the car to go to the game tonight?

Mrs. Anderman was going to do her best to foster this romance. She was tired of his constant moodiness and hoped that a nice girlfriend like Patti would improve his disposition.

"Yea that'd be great." Frank's color was coming back. He was curious but didn't want to question his mother's willingness to surrender the car on this night when a million reasons would be rejected as invalid requests on others.

"Well have it home by 11:00 or yuh won't be gettin it again. Now one of yuh go get some spuds up from the basement, I'm outta them up here. Take the old ones that are sprouting, might as well save as much as I can of em."

Philip surprised them both by jumping up and going after the potatoes without the usual discussion about who had been the last to go after something. He clomped down the stairs as loudly as he had gone up them when his mother had come home. His brother Fred had told him that burglars hid in the dark area between the shelves and the underside of the treads with long rusty bladed knives, just waiting to slit his throat. He always thought about the story when going down by himself for anything, and even though he knew it was just one of the many things Fred had told him that later turned out to be untrue, he still gave the steps a good stomp to keep anything lurking in the dark, back in the shadows.

Fred was thirteen and his budding sexuality kept him awake at night. Unlike Frank who was tortured by the thoughts that pursued him and intruded into every moment of his day, Fred reveled in them. Philip always questioned the amount of time Fred spent in the bathroom and would get shushed for asking. Fred's confessions were quick and his penance quicker. He had learned to lie even about his sins. He was a carefree child.

Philip collected an armful of the white whiskered tubers and went back up the stairs. His pants still dripped water softly onto the concrete floor, but the evidence of his trespassing in the swamp was slowly evaporating. At confession this would be a, "disobeyed my mother and father." He'd probably get two or three Hail Mary's or a couple Our Fathers for it, but at least he wouldn't be grounded for the weekend.

Chapter 3

Under the railroad loading platform, in between Lake Street and Highway 371, down amongst the bundles of oak shims the railroad workers need for leveling tracks, and winos use to lay up in and sleep off binges, four young adolescents sat in a shifting circle bending over and jostling each other for a better view of something held in the shaking hands of the largest of the youth.

"Turn the page Tony. Christ yer so damn slow. Give it to me if yuh can't do it right, we've seen uhnuf uh that ugly whore."

"You'd get the pages all sweaty Fred yer drippin all over an shakin so bad nun of us could see it."

This could have been honestly said about any of the group of young sinners but they only noticed it in their companions. A skinny twelve year old wearing an expensive looking brown plaid shirt and gray trousers looked up from his less handsomely dressed friends and said, "yuh think anybody can see us down here? I'd sure catch hell if some one snitched on us."

His name was Arthur, and he'd borrowed the magazine' (the object of their rapt attentions), from his brothers rather extensive collection. Arthur was the youngest, and by far smallest in the group. To gain acceptance at first, and later to avoid getting beat up, he would take pornography from his brothers well supplied library, and share it with his "friends". Being small and rich in an area where neither quality was admired Arthur had found something that made him popular.

"Oh wow you think a woman would really do somethin like that?"

"Sure, they do it all the time, how yuh think you got here."

"My ma never did nothin like that. Better watch yer mouth Tony or I'll kick yer ass."

Tony snorted his disbelief in the threat, but most were quite sure that their mother had not, and probably could not, have done any of the acts captured in the black and white and occasional color photographs.

This was a very dirty magazine, not like the "Playboys", and "All Males" Art usually smuggled out. This was a foreign one. It showed perfectly normal and necessary acts in such a way that even if their ministers and parents hadn't made sex seem a dirty and shameful act, the pictures would leave them without a vestige of romance attached to reproduction.

"Tony's right, that's how they do it sometimes. My brother John told Tom about that stuff when he came home on leave last spring. I heard em talkin one night an it sounded like they do it just like that." Fred's statement authenticated the pictures, an older brother who was in the service could not be discounted.

In the distance a shrill horn was being blown. This was Fred's signal to head home for dinner, and all the other boys knew that similar demands would soon be made for their presence at supper tables. This session with, "The Ladies of Copenhagen" was ending.

"You get that same magazine tomorrow Art. We'll have it all day an maybe stash it down here so we can come look at it anytime we want to."

"I can't get it. My brothers home from college and he'd miss it for sure."

"Come on Arty, get it or we'll pound yuh."

"I really can't. You guys don't know my brother. If he found out he'd take em all up to school with him and we'd never get none again."

"Could yuh bring somethin else somethin he might not miss, not one uh them "True Detective", somethin with lots a skin."

"I'll try, but don't expect nothin cuz he spends uh lotta time up in that room studyin an stuff on weekends."

"He must come out to take uh crap an eat. Just don't disappoint us Arty, you remember what that's like don't yuh."

Arthur nodded his head as he tucked the coveted magazine inside his shirt.

Fred crossed the tracks and ran up a steep dirt washout where the sandburs didn't grow. He brushed the oak shavings off the seat of his pants and cut across the Slayton's backyard. Tom's rusty forty-nine Hudson was parked in front of his mother's Chevy but the pickup wasn't there so they couldn't be too serious about supper yet.

As he entered the kitchen Philip sat the last of the plates on the table and stuck out his tongue in response to Fred's none to gentle brotherly punch on the shoulder.

"Where is everybody?" Fred asked as he filled the water pitcher from the tap at the sink.

Philip turned from getting the silverware. "Tom and Frank are upstairs getting ready for the game and Ma's over at Slayton's bringin em uh cup uh sugar or somethin."

"Dad said he'd take us to the game if he gets home in time, but yuh better not try hangin round me if we go."

Philip looked up from scraping some egg yolk he'd missed in washing off a fork tine with his fingernail, "Why'd I want to hang round you. Yer friends are such pukes."

"I don't know why, but yer always there buggin me an sayin stupid stuff. So just keep clear uh me."

Philip shrugged, stuck out his tongue when Fred looked in the refrigerator for the butter, and placed the de-yolked fork at Fred's spot, then took the short tined salad fork he'd given him and placed it by Tom's plate. Everybody complained about the short fork but Fred usually had the biggest fit so Philip generally made sure it was there to set him off before each meal.

"Peggy Slayton's gonna have uh baby"

Fred looked up from the brassier add provocatively placed on the fourth page of the new Penny's sales flyer, which he had dug out of the magazine bin in front of the bathroom door. "What's that news to you? I heard bout that only bout a month ago."

"Are you sure Deak was sayin men pee down there to get uh baby started?"

"He said that but he's full uh crap, Arty had this magazine," Fred then paused considered what he was about to say, "Deak don't know nothin."

Philip looked at his brother and sensed there was something being left unsaid, but Fred was disappearing into the bathroom, sales circular clenched in hand, and Philip knew further discussion would be impossible.

In the distance Philip heard his father's pickup down shift and backfire as it turned off the highway, and its muffler-less roar as it crossed the tracks and climbed the hill onto Lake Street. Its brakes squeaked as he pulled up to the curb in front of their house. The engine chugged along dieseling to a final wheezing belch when he popped the clutch with the ignition off and the shifter held tight in first. Mrs. Anderman met him at the curb before he was rounding the front. He poked her in the back with his lunch box in their brief embrace.

"I didn't think you'd ever get home. That woman has more to complain about then anybody I know. The sound of yer truck roundin the corner was like uh reprieve from the governor."

"What's goin on now?"

"Oh mostly the usual. What's Peggy gonna do with the baby? What's everybody sayin bout them? How things would uh just been different if Mr. Slayton sted ah Peggy's real father had died in the war."

"I bet after 17 years uh that crap he wished he had."

"Well she really ain't doin so good an he ain't much help bein gone all the time like he is."

"I think that's what's kept em together so long."

She snorted in agreement transferred the sugar cup to her left hand and caught her husbands hand as it swung by squeezing it for reassurance about their marriage that she didn't find in his joke, or the grin that accompanied it.

"How was work today?"

"Same old crap."

"Did yuh finish the roofing?"

"Nea."

"Goin to the game tonight?"

"Thought I might. Mind if I take the kids off your hands?"

"Nea."

He squeezed her hand, they grinned, and entered the house to assume the responsibilities that were their anchors.

Chapter 4

Stump watched the children leave the loading ramp and waited until they were well away from the area before crossing over the tracks and continuing on his way. He wasn't afraid of what the children would do to him, but when in groups they seemed more likely to tease or pull tricks, either they felt brave enough to, or not brave enough not to torment. One of the first town skills Stump learned was to avoid packs of children.

Sam Cloud was pulling a 16 foot cedar strip boat onto shore as Stump called out to him. "Leo gave me free beer."

"Uh whole bunch or just the one?"

"Just one."

Sam waited until Stump had grabbed the other side and then finished the job of beaching the heavy boat.

Stump sat on the prow and lit a cigarette. Sam carried a wash tub full of gill net over to his pickup and lifted it into the back. He walked back and started bailing water out of the boats ribbed bottom.

"So why yuh suppose Leo give me the beer."

"Oh I don't know cause he's uh great humanitarian," Sam paused briefly, "nea probly not. He must uh asked yuh to do somethin he didn't want to do."

"That's right Sam he ast me to tell yuh he'd like to see yuh bafor dark if I saw yuh. An I knew yuh'd be here gettin yer boat in so I come down."

"Leo say what he wanted."

"Nope, but he was talkin to dem fellas about gettin some fish then he asks me to get yuh an gives me uh beer."

Sam chuckled and said, "Well maybe he is uh Humanitarian after all."

"Grab one uh them washtubs an I'll see if Leo won't spring for another free one for yuh."

Stump grabbed the handles of a wash tub and lifted it and its contents of flopping fish out of the boat. Sam from the other side was doing the same with another tub.

"Can I go with yuh tomorrow mornin and pull net."

"Nea, Goatman's been helpin in the morning, but I could sure use uh hand in the afternoon. It's damn near impossible to pull by yer self, specially if there's any kind'a wind, an he's generally drunk by now, if he's managed to unload the fish I give him for helpin."

"He told me he had to quit cause his gizzard was all screwed up from drinkin sterno."

"I think it's his brain that's all screwed up, says as long as he stays off the hard stuff he's ok. Meanwhile he pukes up organs every time he goes out with me."

"Now I'll take one uh them smokes you were so kind to offer when I was up to my elbows in fish slime." Sam finished washing his hands in the lake, wiped them on his pant legs and took the cigarette Stump extended to him. He lit it with a Zippo lighter that had a little parachute with silver wings on it.

"Now let's go do some business."

Stump waited as Sam slid across the front seat of the pickup and opened the door.

"When yuh gonna get uh new handle, bet yuh Bert Gardner would have one in his junk yard?"

"Think so huh? Spose Bert would take a whitefish for trade cause I ain't puttin another dime into this thing. Besides anyone in too much uh hurry to wait for me to open it should be riding with someone else."

"Might take two whitefish yuh want me to ask?"

"What you my business agent now? I spose yer gonna want the same cut Leo gets."

"I don't want nothin. Why's Goatman gettin so crazy again? He got him an apartment an don't have to live with them goats no more. He don't hardly even stink much no more, cept when he messes himself from gettin too drunk."

Sam was used to sudden changes in topics, "Goatman needed them goats, and livin out in that old shack kept him outta town so he either had to take uh bottle home or just get drunk once in uh while. Now he can get drunk whenever. They should uh just let him go back out there last time they let him outta the loony bin. He's gonna drink himself to death either way, but this'll be lots quicker."

"What's Leo mean bout Comyanists? He said Glen was talkin like one when they were goin on about the game warden. Goatman said he was uh comyanist one time, said that's why they keep puttin him away."

"Goatman ain't no communist, anarchist maybe, next time he has uh bottle ask him for half of it then you'll see what kind'a communist he is."

Stump thought this over and smiled thinking of what would happen if he asked for a share of liquor from his animal loving friend. He looked out a cracked side window and watched the town slide by. People were doing their evening shopping, hurrying home from work to start weekending in various manners. Goatman staggered out of the municipal liquor store protectively clutching a narrow brown bag to his chest. Other customers did the same, but not from fear of being hit up for a swallow. Stump waved wildly at his friend, who recognizing the vehicle and occupants, shuffled quickly down a side alley and out of sight. Mr. Patterson, the attorney, not recognizing either, and thinking he was being acknowledged, waved cordially, and tucked his pint of "Five Star" into an overcoat pocket.

Sam turned into the alley Goatman had entered, and Goatman hearing the truck follow, ducked into the trash filled slot between the Lakeshore Hotel and Baudette's Cafe. Sam smiling continued to drive and parked his pickup behind the VFW.

"You want me to go get Leo?"

"Nea I wanna make sure there ain't no cops or wardens in there. For some reason they think they can tell me what to do with my own fish."

Sam rang the service buzzer which could be heard in the darkness of the storage room. A short time later a muffled curse was heard, and then a single naked light bulb was illuminated mid-room by Leo, who could be seen wiping his hands on an apron that had gained stains since Stump had seen it last. He walked the narrow alley between beer kegs and stacked case lots of bottled beer and other provisions to the wire covered rear door. He peered out at them through the dirty window and drew the bolt.

"How you fellers doin?" he said, as he wiped his hands again.

"Not too bad. Stump said yuh wanted to see me."

"Yep got some fellers askin for fish. Said they'd take all the Walleyes yuh could come up with."

"Don't have any, gotta big snake but I already promised Gramma Jones I'd bring her the next one I got. She likes to boil em with spuds an carrots. Good way to ruin all three but who's to say. Got about thirty whitefish all of em hump backs."

"Shit! These feller was ready to pay two bucks apiece for walleyes."

"Yea I'm sure they were. These are dandy fish buck apiece gets em not a cent less."

Leo walked to the end of Sam's pickup and dragged a washtub to the side where he could see in better. The fish were all between four and seven pounds and had the distinctive humped back coming down to a tiny head that mature whitefish have. The smell of fish was overpowering.

"God they sure smell like whitefish. I'd give yuh fifty cents apiece for the whole damn bunch of em."

Sam laughed and shook his head. "Leo yuh damn crook you'll smoke em an sell em for three. I don't mind uh guy makin uh buck but I'd just as soon not having him pick it outta my pocket. Yuh want em they're uh buck. If yuh don't I gotta be goin."

Leo sighed as if some where deep down inside he had a secret pain but reached for his wallet and pulled out a twenty and a ten.

"Say Stump if yuh wanna make uh couple bucks yuh can clean them fish for smokin, split em down the back. You done that before ain't yuh."

Stump nodded his head, thought a second and said, "Five, for five bucks, them's uh lotta fish Leo."

"Christ I ain't gonna make uh dime off this deal. I'll bring yuh uh tub to stick the clean ones in an uh knife. Make sure yuh get all the guts out even the blood up along the rib cage."

Sam stepped up into the bed of the pickup and dug down to the bottom of the fullest tub and pulled out a large northern pike and stuffed it into a near by burlap bag. He jumped back down and started dumping the remaining fish out on the ground near a rack containing several garbage cans. Leo had disappeared into the storage room but was rattling around in search of the promised tools.

"See I told yuh if yuh ask for uh fair price you'll get it. I know Leo's good to yuh but it's uh lotta work slabbing all them fish. Don't be doin it for nothin."

Stump grinned at his friend and pulled the lid from one of garbage cans. "I'm gonna do this next summer when the launch guys try to get me to clean fish for uh dime apiece."

Sam drove off as Stump dreamed of the money he would make in the following summer.

Leo came out with a galvanized tub and a stout bladed butcher knife, and then left Stump to his work.

Stump picked one of the slimy silver fish up from the pile, and placed it on the lid of the can next to the one he had removed the lid from, and with a slow deliberate stroke removed the head. As he started the cut down the spine he heard some rattling in between the next two buildings as Goatman stepped out of the shadows.

He walked over and sat down next to the doorway Leo had just disappeared into, reached up and tried the doorknob, finding it locked he leaned back against the wall and studied his working friend with a curious eye.

"If you would give me the five Leo pays for cleaning that mess uh fish I could buy us uh bottle."

"What yuh do with the one yuh just had."

"I dropped it back there an it broke, inferior glass, I remember when uh bottle of good wine could take uh little jostlin." He laughed lightly and by himself at his small joke.

Stump looked at him wondering when and how the next stab at his as yet unearned five would come. "I bet that jug was empty when it hit the ground."

"Yer gettin too cynical Stump, it don't go with the otherwise kind attitude you always show'd me."

"I already had two beers an my worker said I been doin real good not drinkin or gettin in trouble."

"Yea. I saw our excellent young civil servant leaving the Lake Shore Villa today. What words uh wisdom did he have to share other than, "Stay Away From Alfred", as much as I hate bein named after the company I used to keep its better'n hearin him call me Alfred."

"He said if I saw yuh to tell yuh he needs to have yuh sign some papers."

"Fuck him! Last time I signed anything for those assholes I was locked up for uh year. He always says the same old shit, "Did You Take Your Lithium Alfred? Did You Get Your Thorazine This Morning?, Have You Heard Anything People Around You Didn't Appear To Hear?", how the fuck am I sposed to know what those round me hear or don't hear. I don't even give uh shit what they hear or if they hear as far as that goes. Hear! Hear!" With that said he pulled the allegedly broken bottle from beneath his coat, toasted the eloquence of his words and sat soaking up the last of the day's Sun, contemplating other approaches to separating Stump from at least a portion of his money.

Stump knowing the futility in arguing with Alfred continued cleaning fish.

Chapter 5

Mr. Anderman's pickup clicked and gurgled as it cooled. An empty grain truck roared as it shifted gears and turned onto Highway 34 and headed back to Fargo. A green liquid dripped into a small puddle beneath the Hudson's radiator. The air smelled of burning leaves, and the rancid mint odor of skunk that clung to the low slung front end of the half-bubble shaped car.

The front door of the house across the street opened a crack. A woman looked down the street, and shut the door again. The shades were drawn and the brief glimpse anyone watching would have gotten of her as she peered out suggested illness or sorrow.

Mrs. Slayton's life had not been full of joy. She had married Henry Slayton after a short drunken romance with a man who had gone off to the war in 1942. He had left her pregnant, single, and with an address that got her letters out of town, but left her mired at home collecting the pleas for help that returned stamped with an inky denial of his existence, with each returned letter she drank more. Whether he had died or lied she would never know. Henry had come along at a convenient time and "rescued" her.

Mrs. Slayton had been honest about her indiscretion, and Henry seemed open minded about the entire matter, claiming it was just the times they lived in, and how his love for her was all that counted. Things were never right for them. She was a good looking women and he had a large nose with a profusion of long hairs poking out of it. His bristly mustache did little to conceal them and gave him even more of a terrier like look. The children of the neighborhood joked endlessly about this physical trait and the job he had chosen, selling "Fuller Brush" products, door to door.

Mr. Slayton never trusted his wife, and didn't have any love for her daughter. Fortunately Peggy was their only child. Fear of an even greater emptiness was all that maintained the household. In their combined misery the one consistency was a nearly silent war fought in three to four word sentences conveying demands or insipient questions which meant something other than what they asked and never developed beyond that.

The Slayton's rejoined the battle, as if uninterrupted, when Henry returned from his week long forays against the world of bored women, who took his small sample packets, and begrudgingly bought an occasional toilet or vegetable brush, and perhaps a bottle of polish. He bragged a lot about life on the road. He always had a new story for sharing of his success with lonely housewives who gave him their favors and sighed as he went on his way. The men he met in bars would listen as long as he was buying the drinks and when he stopped paying they left him to the unfortunate bartender until reprieve came and the tavern closed. In the seedy motel rooms he shared with an occasional prostitute he developed new stories and savored the bitterness of his life. He would nod at Mr. Anderman from the curb as he unloaded his suitcase and sample box from the station wagon, smiling as if in a shared confidence, jut his hips in a suggestive manner, and walk into his house where endless battle over unforgiven sins went on into eternity.

Peggy had grown tired of this along with Henry's eyes and busy hands. She lived in an apartment above Baudette's Cafe with a friend whose reputation was as tarnished as her own. Her self image had always been poor, but at one time she had tried to fit into the town's somewhat confusing moral standards. With her pregnancy she had given up. She flaunted her wickedness, wearing clothes and makeup that drew stares and disapproving clucks, and validated the worst of the stories about her by entertaining openly in her room. Peggy destroyed the little self respect she had been able to develop growing up surrounded by her mother's dreams of a world that had never been, and her step-father's blaming finger. She was eighteen and sure she was less afraid of death than she feared an unchanged life. So she waited tables downstairs, unsuccessfully exorcised demons upstairs, and found what little salvation she could in the fantasy world her mother had prepared her for.

Mrs. Slayton sat on the edge of her unmade bed and contemplated the empty brandy bottle. It would be just like Henry to come home without her weekly bottles. He forgot it deliberately, she knew that. He'd get to make a big deal of having to go back out after a week on the road, and say something about two quarts not lasting as long as they used to. Each word would reinforce that she was nothing without him, and that all she had depended on his continued existence in her life. Out on the street she heard a car pull up in front of the house and stop. She lay back down, turned her head to the wall, and closed her eyes to the sound of an opening door.

Henry knew where she was, and that the noise from every move he made was being assessed. He sloshed the bottles gently as he sat them on the dining room table. She was by his side before he could put his sample case in the hall closet.

"Figgered if I picked em up first we could get the drinkin an fuckin done before we sit an stare at each other."

"Why do yuh say such trash? Can't yuh just come home an be nice."

"I could if there was uh meal waitin an you looked like yuh been outta bed for more then five minutes in the whole day."

She eyed the bottle, and decided to go along with the evening he had suggested when he arrived, and ignore his words, for now. Reaching into the china hutch she pulled out two small glasses and poured them full from the bottle he had opened.

The longing for a normal life was hard to put away. "So how was things out on the road?"

"Lotta fuckin difference it makes to you."

She made a small face and with a shaking hand picked up her glass.

Chapter 6

Dinner at the Anderman house was a noisy affair. Though a good deal speedier with only Philip to pester into cleaning up his plate, it still consumed a large portion of an hour with the flurry of conversation of the day's happenings to discuss.

"Pass them spuds Frank."

"Did we get any mail today Ma?"

"Got some, nothin good. John wrote, sent some pictures of his ship, said cuz uh things goin on over there he ain't gonna get leave in December. Probly won't come home till summer now." Mrs. Anderman's eyes watered as she said this and an awkward silence fell over the table. Displays of emotion other than joy or anger were unusual in their home. With John in the Navy they would spend the first Christmas without the whole family together. "We gotta bill from the power an light, an uh letter from the Church askin for money to help educate more Priests ."

Mr. Anderman laughed, "Somebody must uh figured we was the rich Anderman's, the ones that have lots to give away."

"Which ones is that? Must be uh side uh the family I don't get to meet."

"What did ole lady Slayton have to say Ma?"

"She's Mrs. Slayton, Fred, an she said you boy's been playin down by the tracks under that platform every night after school. Better not be hookin rides on the freights. More then one boys been killed playin round trains. Mr. Slayton's sposed to be here tonight, some time, he's having uh fit bout this baby comin, blames it all on her of course, says she was always so easy on the girl."

At the mention of the railroad platform Fred blushed. When Peggy's situation was brought up Tom looked down at his plate and went to work on his piece of liver with feigned interest, and a slight smirk.

"We goin to the game tonight Dad? You said we could if yuh got home in time." Philip said this after he had successfully stashed a spoonful of peas under the edge of his plate.

Both Fred and Philip were of the opinion that there was plenty of time. Fred added, "Ma's got the Ladies Brotherhood here tonight anyway so it'll give yuh an excuse to get away from that."

The group he mentioned was actually The Ladies Study Society, but Mr. Anderman had renamed it, and for the boys it would always be, the Ladies Brotherhood. Labels didn't matter much, other peoples misfortunes were the prime focus of study, and when something particularly toothsome was being "studied", they didn't sound much like ladies. Mrs. Slayton's request for sugar had come at a perfect time for Mrs. Anderman. She now had the latest on that tragedy, and more on the eternal saga of the Slayton's in general.

Mrs. Slayton knew that what she said wouldn't be kept a secret, and in fact counted on the fact that it wouldn't be. She loved the, "You poor things", she was lavished with, and craved the company. Even when Peggy had been in the house she had acted a ghost; never seen if Henry was home, and a fleeting specter that occasionally stopped to ask for money, or to sign a note excusing her absence from school during her husbands blessed days away. That was before she quit school and moved out. The kindness of neighbors was Mrs. Slayton's link to the world now, that and Henry's weekend's home. She gladly and needfully dumped her sorrows out on anyone that would take the time to listen. And they in turn shared these harrowing tales, and all felt that their lives were somewhat less mediocre, they were perhaps even blessed. Mrs. Anderman came away with as much as she left.

"Say Tom, that Hudson's gotta leak. Looks like yer loosing antifreeze. Might have uh bad hose or somethin."

"Oh crap! I knew somethin was wrong. It smelled hot tonight comin home, an Sam Cloud told me it sounded like it had uh bad water pump last week."

"Did it squeak, usually they squeak when the pumps goin."

"Yea it squeaked some, but if yuh turned up the radio yuh couldn't hear it no more, so I figgered it wasn't too serious."

His father shook his head in disbelief, "Well with any luck yuh didn't hurt it, better leave it where it sits till yuh get uh chance to slap uh new one in."

"Can I take the Chevy?"

Mrs. Anderman spoke up before Frank choked on his liver. "No you can't Frank already asked for it for his date."

Tom looked happily at his younger brother. "Who you takin out Frankie?"

"Patti Richardson!"

"She ain't too bad. Little chubby for my taste but seems to be uh nice kid."

Frank was about to take exception to the chubby part of his brothers comment, but decided that it would only get worse, and he might even open himself up to more of the none too gentle of a ribbing he could expect from all of his brothers.

Tom sensing his error changed the subject. "How bout givin me uh ride to the game before yuh pick her up?"

Frank nodded affirmatively and doused his potatoes with more gravy.

"Yuh wanna ride home with me an the boys Tom?"

"Nea! I'll get one of the guys to give me uh lift."

"You make sure to come home right after the game, yer spending too much time chasing round lately. Bout time yuh spent some time home at night." Mrs. Anderman could see her speech would go unheeded. Tom had gone too far too long to be brought in now. She was looking forward to his leaving home after graduation. She hoped the other boys weren't picking up on his ability to get what he wanted with so little given in return. Her feelings for him were as great as it was for the other boys, but she hated the casual way he had of using people, it reminded her of his father not so long ago.

An unseen signal passed between the two older boys. Tom stood up and walked to the door, pulling his jacket off the hook he turned to his mother.

"Good supper Ma! I might be just uh little late. Bunch of the guys were talkin bout stoppin somewhere for uh pop, but I'll try to get outta there as quick as I can but, since I'm ridin it might be late."

"You can always ride home with yer Dad. Or God forbid walk home!"

Tom glanced at Frank who was practicing smiles in the kitchen mirror, once again a signal was exchanged and both boys headed out the door.

As the boys left the house Mrs. Anderman could feel her world slowly being filled with shadows. Each would in turn leave creating voids much larger than simple seating places deserted at her table. She didn't know what her life would be without a daily regimen of responsibilities to take care of. Her daily visits to ladies like Mrs. Slayton whose children were gone and lives seemed so empty reinforced these fears. Hearing the car start shook her from the melancholy.

"I hope yer plannin on eatin them peas, cuz they sure won't grow where yer planting em."

Philip looked up, tried an innocent expression, realized he was caught and spooned the offensive vegetables into his mouth. He then made a production out of washing them down with a large gulp of water.

Chapter 7

"You got any gum?"

Tom reached into his pocket and pulled out a nearly empty pack of Double Mint. He tore the lone stick of it in half, measured the pieces and gave the smaller chunk to his brother.

"Thanks! You the one that did Peggy?"

"No fuckin way! I don't go in without the right equipment." He reached into the same pocket he'd pulled the gum from and held up several foil wrapped condoms.

"Yuh want one for tonight?"

"She ain't like that. She's not one of yer pumps."

Tom glanced over at Frank. "Look Frankie, they all aren't pumps. I'm just tellin yuh, things get goin, an yuh get carried away, an even nice girls will put out, an if that happens yuh use one of these. I know uh bunch uh guys that are shittin their pants right now bout Peggy, with one uh these no sweat." To emphasize his point he casually slid back in his seat and looked out the side window of the Chevy.

"What would yuh do if Ma found those in yer pocket? She'd have uh shit fit!"

"Hell, she'd probly be relieved, least she'd quit givin me the snake eyes every time somebody mentions Peggy Slayton."

"What yuh think I should act like tonight, yuh know with Patti? I don't know what to say, Christ everything seems so stupid after I say it, then next thing yuh know, I'm talkin dumb agin."

Tom laughed, "Yer problem is yuh talk too deep, feed her a line, girls don't give a shit bout books, an what you think is wrong with the world. Ask if she watched Father Knows Best or some crap on TV, then act like yer payin attention to what she says. Give em uh chance and they'll do most of the talkin."

"No! That's when we talk the best is about books. I guess she likes music too, but I don't know much except what's on the radio. She's always talkin about how the Beatles are so great."

"Well agree with her then and don't get so nervous. Cindy says Patti's got the hots for you, always lookin at yuh in the hall, an askin if any bodies seen yuh, don't sweat it, you got it made."

Frank didn't reply but smiled as he drove around the back of the school.

Tom reached back into his pocket and pulled out one of the prophylactics. "Frank, I'm serious take this, if yuh don't need it now yuh might some other time. It ain't worth screwin round an bein stuck in this hole just cuz yuh knocked some chick up an can't leave town. Think of all them poor bastards workin their asses off for the rest of their lives, supporting uh wife an kids. Not me I'm gettin the hell outta here." He turned the rear view mirror to the right and briefly admired what he saw there. As he stepped out of the car he dropped the condom on the passenger seat.

"See yuh in the mornin."

Frank looked at the object and then outside at the parking lot. No one was there.

He picked it up and hesitantly examined it. He squeezed it lightly, an energy seemed to flow out of it into his hand causing his stomach to churn, not unlike the feeling he had when he was doing something he knew he would have to confess. He looked around again and then reached down and pulled out his thin wallet. He slipped the condom into a side pouch like he'd seen other boys in school do, behind the picture flaps. Frank shifted the Chevy into reverse and backed slowly out onto the street. He could feel the strange bump in his wallet and wiggled around a bit to accustom himself to it, shifted again, then drove down the hill, across the tracks, and towards Patti's house.

Chapter 8

The game was a way of life for small towns. Each sent out the biggest and fastest of its splotchy faced gladiators to do battle for the honor of the home folk. Strategies were much discussed. A teacher stuck with coaching depended on success for his livelihood. After a bad season a coach often was terminated and went on to another town to be the scapegoat or the hero depending upon the size and skill of the crop of young men assigned to him.

Dusty cars would pull up the hill and park as close to the field as possible, wheels turned to the curb, stubborn doors slammed. Families walked through the dead weeds up to the edge of the field where the mettle of one town would be set against that of another. Men and women, old from long hours, put in more hours standing behind the ropes that hedged the arena, watching a son or brother go against those by the opposite ropes sons and brothers. Wrapped in parkas they waited the outcome and sucked down coffee prepared by whatever club ran the concession stand. On the hills above couples sat and children played. Gusts of breath mix with the steam of hot beverages and search out stars in the cold blue sky. Above the field, lights burn, illuminating the pageant below with electricity's impartiality. In the shadows young lovers whisper of things they can't understand. By the field their parents dream of times they can't re-live and try to forget things they understood only too well. The gaps between what will be, what was, and dreams kept the spirit of the game alive.

Boys and girls ran in and out of the sumac bushes. With milkweed stalk swords they hacked at each other as one side pushed the other towards the sand bank. Screaming and laughing, occasionally they would watch the game, but it didn't hold their interest in the midst of unsupervised bedlam.

During half time the children rushed down to their parents to beg change for hot chocolate, candy and if "lucky" enough a hot dog. The aroma of coffee was as rich an odor as had ever passed nostrils on those autumn evenings. It was part of the elixir that brought the town out. On cold nights the mud churned up by afternoon practice would freeze into an uneven platform where theories could be rehashed about games and players of the past. The aging heroes would smile at mention of their name or deeds, and correct any errors that detracted from past glories. They seemed to resent when a child would shake them from reverie of their youth, and drag them back to responsibilities of the day with requests for money, or complaints of the cold.

Some of the men carried flasks of minty smelling liquor. They passed them off to friends as they talked. The clear liquid bubbled, the friend would gasp a bit and wink their thanks before passing it back.

On the hill above the field Frank sat holding the hand of a girl draped in his coat.

"Are you sure yer warm, cuz I'm really OK?

"Nea, I don't feel cold at all!"

Shadowed from the overhead lights she couldn't see the shivers that made a liar of him, or spoke to the effect her nearness created in his lean frame. Conversations had started and died a dozen times in the short while they'd sat there. When he captured her hand she felt the unfortunate urge to recall a story of how she'd recently needed a wart burned off that very hand. He dropped the hand thinking she was making a comparison of the two. She retrieved the hand in the dark and gently squeezed his fingers.

Now they sat watching the game in pretended interest while their minds developed things to say that they couldn't voice.

He contemplated putting his arm around her and she wondered what to do when he did. The cold handled the matter for them.

"You are shivering!" She could feel the trembling even in his hand.

"No really I'm fine."

She reached behind him and felt his back which was cold to the touch.

"Here put yer jacket back on an put yer arm round my back, then we'll both be warm."

He did as requested. A cold breeze came up off the lake and they snuggled together for greater warmth. In the distance a dog barked and another answered. The ball moved back and forth on the field, the crowd yelled encouragement.

The children grew tired of their play. Many stood by the side lines in submission to a sports mania they couldn't understand. They asked questions and annoyed their fathers until the final whistle blew and the players ran off the field, to a locker room filled with yells and excited talk, or to one echoing noisy cleats, and the hushed whispers of blame.

People walked down dark trails to start cold vehicles and begin the stream of lights running down the hill, to homes or to bars, where the business of dissecting this latest game could begin.

Children worn out by the reckless abandon of their recent play were carried limp to bed or nudged into semi-consciousness and led off to sleep. Wives who had stayed home asked a few questions as to outcome, and people seen, half listening to statistics, they too wandered off to the warmth of bed and quilts. Later in the night wheels crunched up drive ways and to curbs as older children returned from dates or parties. Parents would roll over noting the time on radium dials near their heads and either sigh in relief or lay awake and fret the morning arguments.

The streets of the town nearly shut down for the night. Drunks going home in a stupor endangered anything that came in range of their flying wheels. Cats and dogs searched out meals from garbage cans, and made noisy notes of their amorous desires. Skunks came out of the woods to compete with domesticated animals for edible refuse. Evidence of these meetings hung in the air, or stubbornly to the coats of offending pets for days after. Slowly the eastern sky lightened, the air warmed a bit, daytime life stirred, and the town began to move again. People who had to work on Saturday used the toilet and cursed the day.

Chapter 9

When the rising of the sun cast its first awakening rays into the east window of the Lake Shore Hotel, Stump was already stirring. On Saturdays, when the weather was nice he would slip out of town and make the pilgrimage to the old homestead where his parents had tried to earn a living plowing around rocks. He put on his old soiled clothes walked down the worn carpet covered steps and out onto the street.

The coming day was slowly burning off the wispy ghosts of fog. It stuck to low spots and the swamp was a cloud. The shrouded tops of the willows and spruce occasionally appeared in the shifting mist and then just as quickly disappeared.

He walked across the rail yard and past the loading ramp where the boys sometimes hid in the shadows of the stacked shims. He looked up the hill at the Slayton house, the girl wasn't there now, but sometimes she stood in tight thin dresses, with the fabric clinging to her body. The thought hurried Stump along away from the town and the many things that tempted, things that his mother had warned him of. He crossed over the mansion road and down the tracks leading into the woods that bordered most of the village. Occasionally he would stop to look at things that interested him.

In a small lake several miles from town a beaver's wide head and mouthful of sticks plowed up a wide ''v'' on the otherwise placid surface. The rodent dove as it approached the mound of logs and mud near shore. Popping back up minutes later, minus the burden of winter food she had stashed in the deep water feed bed in front of the house, the sleek animal went on with its work.

Stump sat on the black end of the creosoted railroad tie and was warmed by the sun as it claimed ownership of the day. Below him a small group of ring necked ducks, made nervous by hunters, swam safely out of shotgun range, and into the middle of the pond. There they sat bobbing up and down, feeding, and watching, as they were being watched. Twice beavers returned with branches which they tucked away in the growing underwater tangle of brush that meant winter survival for their colony. Stump's addiction finally awake, he lit the first cigarette of the day. His movement alerted the nearest beaver, it smashed its tail loudly down on the water, causing ducks to fly, and the other beaver to disappear.

Stump smiled remembering how his father had taken him along duck hunting. They scanned each slough with a spy glass, his dad letting him look to see what they were after. When Stump had spotted the quarry his father would give directions to wait while he sneaked around the slough, watch for him to wave his hat from a certain point on the other shore, and then to walk noisily up to the pond yelling if need be to make the ducks fly. The startled birds would jump up, and thinking they were making good their escape, fly happily into range of the elder Stump's waiting shotgun. When he was getting old his father let Stump carry the gun, and to shoot it once, but that made his mother angry so he wasn't allowed to do it again. Those were happy days, walking through the woods behind his father, carrying a burlap bag heavy with unfortunate waterfowl. He wondered as he often did why they had had to end.

He stubbed out his cigarette in the cinder sand mixture of the rail bed, stood up, and continued his journey.

On a hill above the tracks an abandoned farm stood. Graying boards from the dilapidated barn twisted in and out from the old wall line, pushed out of place by a roof smashed flat with snow and wind. He had crawled through its hay mow seeking hidden kittens as a child, and later seeking privacy as a teen beset by the horrors of an unexplained puberty. Not far from the barn the foundation of his house lay and in some places stood. Time and weather had been aided in their work by vandals with rocks and matches. Stump walked up the slope onto the edge of a field. He pushed down the rusty barbed wire fence, its post planted years ago by a grandfather he never had known, broke off low by the ground. The rusty staples pulled out and fell into the grass with the bits of punky rotting wood they had been driven into; giving up on their long obedience to the forgotten man who with his hammer had placed them in bondage to a purpose similarly forgotten. The long twisted wire gave out a complaining squeak, as rusty metal dragged across rusty metal in places where staples continued in service to the dead. Stump stepped easily over the fading boundary and walked up by the old buildings.

The late fall flowers were still standing in close to the sheltered southern sides of the old buildings; purple, yellow, and white splotches in the long brown grass. A huge apple tree, disease eating its gnarled limbs, stood where it would always stand in Stumps mind. The ground was littered with apples that had fallen, a few still clung stubbornly to the leafless branches. He sat on the fire charred logs of the house in a hole that had once been the kitchen window. The walls had fallen in, and mice whose ancestors had risked life to live here, now owned the nooks, cracks, and whole of what remained. He picked some apples from the lower limbs and ate them. Frost had made them soft, and the tartness of the little apples made his mouth pucker. His memory registered toast and jelly, and looking out at these same trees from his breakfast plate. Wrapped in his memories he filled his belly with the weathered fruit.

The mice determined him not to be a threat and came out, scurrying and squeaking beneath the carpet of fallen leaves. A glimpse of brown as they crossed over a log or the infrequent spot of bare ground was the only visual evidence of their noisy presence. They gathered acorns from the oaks which had grown there before "development" and now assisted in the process of erasing evidence that there had ever been any. Sensing the snows were coming even mice that had known no winter gathered and stashed food in a scampering race with time. They grew so bold that some forgot about him and passed within inches of his boots. He watched them for a time until he saw the slinking shape of a weasel. His attention then became riveted on the ducking, scooting game of murder and survival that unfolded in front of him. The tiny killer froze by the apple tree as a mouse paused to gnaw on a downed fruit. The weasel pounced, a shrill squeak and the hunter looked up from his kill, and then both disappeared.

Each animal was doing as it was intended to do, filling its niche, and being observed by a member of a species that had thoughts that it was somehow beyond this natural order. All would some day fall to the earth and be swallowed up, enriching the soil, allowing grass to grow, apples to be bitter sweet, and acorns to find spots to take root.

A big buck gray squirrel that had been shuffling through the leaves at the base of an oak, searching for fallen nuts, hearing the scream and struggle of death, ran back up into the safety of the tree. He chattered and barked looking at the big man on the old wall blaming him for the disturbance. Stump remained silent, and waited the return of tranquility, where memories came so easily. In the distance a horn sounded and then traffic noise from a passing vehicle on Highway 34 .

His parents and grandparents had spent most of the precious hours of their lives tending these fields, building, and later repairing this house and barn. A tree grew from the old foundation and absorbed the sweat of men and women who had tried to change the land while it shaped them. The hours of endless labor had bent their backs, killed the men and driven his mother away. In town she would at times sit in the sun and warm her wrinkles, at last relieved of the hard work, she had time to reflect on the beauty of what had passed. She eventually sold the land to a neighbor. He left the buildings to decay, and only came here to cut hay on the lower fields, where the rocks didn't dismantle his tractor when he worked the land. Stump was the only person to come here to watch time pass by this little patch of hard woods that had protected a boy named Carl from the winter wind, and summer sun.

In the woods by the big swamp a grouse drummed out a song of love and territory. A noisy vehicle slowed and then stopped down by the road. An iron gate the new owner had put up squeaked as it opened, and then the noise came nearer. Tires churning in the half frozen mud, and gears grinding, a blue flat bed truck approached the lower field. Stump walked back to the fence and hid in the sumac to watch what was going on from a place where he wouldn't be seen. The truck stopped by a tarp covered pile of hay bales. An old man climbed down from the driver's side and another man jumped lightly out of the passenger's side. He stretched lazily and looked curiously long at the sumacs. The older man walked to the hay and rolled back the log that held the tarps edge down from the wind. He owned the field, and the hay, the dilapidated farm, and even the sumacs where Stump now lay. His name was Anson and he too was pouring out his sweat to nourish trees he would never stop to see. The two men pulled back the rest of the tarp revealing neatly stacked greenish bales of hay. Mice that had thought this a good place to spend the winter scrambled in search of cover in the stubble, leaving their stores of seeds and acorns to be kicked aside by the men who didn't care about the hours wasted collecting them.

Backs bent to the task, they grabbed the twine bound bales with gloved hands and strained, lifting the bundles of fodder onto the truck which bounced and sank with each added burden tossed on top of the other. When the truck would hold no more they tied down the load with long ropes. The old man got in and said something to the younger man who then also climbed in. The engine whirred and then caught, roared briefly, then ran smoothly as the truck turned and rolled down the rutty road towards the highway.

When it had quieted Stump returned to his seat in the old window sill and ate a few more apples. Eventually the squirrels came out of hiding and the mice redoubled their efforts to renew the destroyed larders. Amongst the generations of Butternut and Maxwell House coffee tins saved to store the odd pieces of life, and then abandoned to rust into oblivion, Stump passed his day. He moved about in his memories picking things up and then lovingly setting them back down. When the truck returned to carry off the rest of the hay, he walked down to the cedar grove by the old well and watched as the men worked.

In the distance the grouse resumed its drumming and cars could be heard going back and forth bound for duty and appointments. His stomach churning for something more than apples or because of them, he decided to go back to town. Stump paused by the railroad embankment and looked back a last time at his home, then slipped over the edge and walked away.

Above, the sun moved on even though it was immobile in the man's mind. In its shifting light the autumn flowers were like spots in the pattern of an ever changing carpet; the bright bits of color that separated brown from gray, what was awake from what had gone to sleep.

Chapter 10

Sam looked up from his clean, folded nets. It was getting late, if Stump didn't hurry up he would have to pull the set nets alone again, and in the wind that was a hard and dangerous job. He sat on the lowered tail gate of his pickup and smoked a cigarette. Watching towards town he waited.

The first indication he had of his tardy friend's presence was the flip flopping of his boot heel coming from the west. Turning his head he could see a half running Stump coming down the tracks, he waived at him and yelled, "For Chrisesake don't have uh heart attack."

Stump slowed to a quick walk and approached Sam with a silly grin.

"I thought for sure yuh would uh took'd off an left me, forgot bout helpin yuh till my guts got to growlin,"

"Been out to the old place?" Stump nodded his head, "well let's shove off or we'll be messing round out there in the dark."

They slid the long wooden boat into the icy water. Sam held it steady as Stump clambered in. He jumped over the edge just before his boots came in contact with lake and scrambled to the back of the boat. Stump sat passively on the middle seat.

"Yuh gonna just be cargo this trip or yuh wanna row?"

Stump thought a second, smiled and took up the oars. With long powerful strokes he propelled the craft into deeper water as Sam primed the small green outboard motor. The motor started on the first pull, its tiny propeller sent the boat slowly but steadily into the waves. The two men were silent, both wrapped in thoughts of irretrievable pasts, they watched as the cold gray water slipped by.

Sam remembered cold days helping his father run nets under the ice with long poles, days when the fish meant survival, not just a way to supplement the unemployment money he received from a construction job that kept him on the road all summer. The rhythmic thumping of explosions inside the two cylinders, the slap of the waves on the boats sides were like a tonic that brought him back to autumns of his youth. He looked back and thought of days soon to come when he would be able to take his boys out netting or ricing and give them an anchor to root them. He nodded his head at Burt Magoo and his wife as their boats passed. Returning from checking their own nets, Burt's woman Sarah shook her head sadly. This reinforced Sam's premonition of empty nets.

They skirted a stand of tall bulrushes and a dozen gulls took flight with a chorus of protesting squawks. The birds circled effortlessly after their labored takeoff and settled back in the same sheltered spot.

As he neared the floating line of buoys that marked his net Sam cut the engine and momentum carried them quietly forward.

"Start rowing again, just ease me in backwards to the first float there, that's it, yer doin real good. Now just take us down long side the net, be careful now don't get too close." Sam peered into the clear water, his eyes confirming what the floating buoys had suggested. Fish in the net usually pulled down, and at least some of the corks should have been submerged. When they had checked the entire length of the net he looked up at a disappointed Stump.

"Well crap, some days are like this an some ain't."

"Yuh gonna move it?"

"Nea, I'll leave it here another night. This day time netting doesn't always pay off but nights usually do."

Stump smiled. He didn't much care for setting net, just the checking of them, and the mystery of what the water might give up. Sometimes a huge wadded ball of net meant a northern pike had happened into it, or looking down as he rowed, he would see flashing bluish silver sided whitefish, they didn't give up the struggle until you cleaned them. Walleyes just stiffened out and lay there in motionless submission to whatever fate had in store for them. He liked the whitefish best, rolled up northern frustrated his friend, and walleyes made for a nervous return to shore. His grumbling stomach reminded him of the missed meals of the day. It was good not to have to go through the tedium of pulling, and resetting the long gill net.

By the time they rounded the point that sheltered the place where Sam kept his boat it was nearly dark. The town's lights twinkled here and there as people turned them on for the night. It was so cold both men were bunched up trying to conserve what little body heat they had after their boat ride.

They were busy pulling the boat up on shore when they realized they weren't alone.

"Mind my seeing whatcha got there Sam?" Al Hoger stood in the gathering gloom by the end of Sam's pickup. He didn't need a badge or uniform, every boy or man in the area that had ever picked up a rod and reel, or gun knew who he was, and that if they became too blatant, or wasteful in harvesting of wild game, they would have an expensive meeting with him.

Sam, startled at first, laughed. "Yuh gotta warrant Al?"

"I sure don't. Must uh left it at home." The game warden switched on a large flashlight and focused its beam on the empty washtubs and then under the seats and around the floor of the boat. "No luck eh!"

"Nea been perty slow, don't seem much point in even settin net this year." Sam fumbled with his stiff fingers to light a cigarette but his lighter seemed to be out of fuel.

Hoger extended a Zippo of his own and lit the cigarette. "Been hearin stuff bout fish gettin sold, you ain't heard nothin like that I spose." The two men being questioned remained silent. "No I didn't think yuh would of. Well if yuh do, make sure to tell whoever's been doin that, that I don't mind people takin a dead game fish home if its dumb enough to get caught in a net, the damn things always seem to die anyways, but I'd have to run somebody in if they happened to be gettin so many of them illegal fish that they had to sell em, stead of eatin em, or given em away to poor widow women. Well you fellas have uh nice night now an try to get warm, feels like some weather might be movin in." With those words the easygoing officer got in his car, started it, and waved goodbye as he drove away.

Sam grinned at Stump. "Some times it's hard to tell when yer havin good luck."

"Yuh think Hoger's uh comyanist?"

"Where the hells all this communist stuff coming from?"

"When Leo was talkin to Glen bout how much walleyes costs, Leo said sumpthin bout Glen bein one, then Glen said he din't think Hoger was, but I don't know now cuz Hoger's goin roun scarin folks an that's just what dem comyanist do."

"Nea, Glen an Leo just talk too damn much, an that's why Hoger has to go out an do his job. Otherwise he'd just sit at home on uh cold night like tonight, an watch TV, stead uh missing supper an bothering me."

At the mention of food Stumps belly let out an audible growl. Stump giggled, "Sounds just like Mrs. Berg's cat when it wants to go out side to make more babies."

"You ate anything yet today?"

"Just uh bunch uh apples. Ellen makes tator soup today an she saves uh bowl for me, so I gotta get goin bafor she gets mad at me."

"Yuh wanna ride?"

Stump's darkness disappeared in the gloom with a muffled refusal, and Sam was left alone by the noisy lake. He reached into his parka pocket and dug around, finally extracting a small pouch. Squatting down he sifted a pinch of tobacco into the freezing waves and smiled sadly at the thought of what his father might say about gifting a lake for not giving up any fish.

The protesting sounds of his own stomach reminded him that Rita was keeping a supper warm at home, and would be worried about the lateness and the wind. He walked to the stern of the boat and shook the motor up and down slightly. The sloshing gasoline assured him that he could make at least one more trip to check the net before he needed to bring the can from home and fill the tiny reservoir on top the engine.

The pickup door squeaked, he pumped the gas petal up and down and tried the ignition, it groaned, sputtered, popped, and finally roared as he let out a whining clutch and left the deserted beach to the work of the waves.

The shreds of tobacco slapped back and forth to the wind and the action of the water, some mixing with the sand on shore, and some sinking gradually, drifting off to appease a Creator that sometimes withholds.

Chapter 11

Stump's pace was awkward on the unevenly spaced ties. The moon coming up caused the rails to glitter on ahead like a twin tracked mirror, partially catching, and reflecting the pale orb. It guided him towards town, towards supper and bed. Light poured out of windows marking the outskirts of town. Homes filled with people who moved about allowing Stump snapshots of dinners being finished. Families settling down in front of television sets which added a flickering show house effect to the scenes that they teasingly offered Stump as he walked by.

He reached the VFW Club just as a group walked out. He stepped aside into the shadows as they passed. The bar was nearly empty. Alfred the Goat Man held court to a disinterested Leo up front. In the corner booth two old women were sipping coffee. After the brief stare that informed them that Stump wasn't an "out of towner" and at least on this night not worthy of further assessment, they returned to their whispering and secretive glances towards the back.

Under a plastic light shade advertising Hamm's Beer, a girl in tight jeans and a Levi jacket played pool with another girl similarly dressed. They both burned filtered cigarettes which hung carelessly from the corners of their mouths, the smoke rising into eyes that teared and squinted. Nearly empty Coke bottles were perched on the sides of the table. Circular white rings and charred black lines on the dark wooden rails were evidence that this wasn't the first time the second and third of many rules taped to the wall by the cue rack had been broken.

The prettier of the two mimicked her less fortunate, and somewhat older friend. Each laugh, the way she stood, even the casual flick of her wrist that sent the ash from her cigarette to the floor an out of synch reflection.

Stump watched her and his face turned red. He looked away. His mother had impressed this lesson on him, and the one mistake he had made reinforced it, stay away from girls; looking at her chipped away at this foundation of his freedom.

"Hey Leo bring us uh Coke."

"What's wrong with yer legs? Don't look broke to me."

"Nea, they ain't broke. You should know that, the way yuh been lookin at em all night. Yuh wanna closer look bring us uh pop an knock off the crap."

Leo shook his head and opened two Cokes. He carried them back to the girls and collected some change from their table. The two women in the booth glanced at each other, silently sharing their disapproval, both of what the girl had said, and that men Leo's age gawked at the body parts of girls who were little more than children.

Lorna Dobbs finished her first soda, handed the empty bottle flirtatiously to Leo, and then shot at the three ball in the corner. She missed, slammed the cue down on the table and swore breaking both rule number five and seven of the conveniently posted laws.

Peggy Slayton also swore. Peggy had a smear of red lipstick in the same shade as her friends. Lacking the artistry of Lorna's application it still had the same basic affect or effect depending on whether you were the wearer or an observer.

They played the game with passion and energy but no skill, taking long serious pauses to study their shots, chalking their cue tips after their accidental successes, outbursts of profanity after the routine misses. Peggy's attempts at mirroring her friend obviously pleased Lorna, who smiled with each awkward vulgarity echoed and relished the scrutiny placed on her every move. Experience had taught her that Peggy's looks attracted men and that occasionally they had friends who couldn't wait for Peggy to be unoccupied. Often they didn't find her totally unattractive, at least at the moment, and for a while her loneliness was lessened. The two girls fed from each others needs; Lorna's need to have men pay some attention to her, Peggy's need for someone to use her for something other than sex. Lorna for all her faults was as close to a friend as Peggy had ever had.

Lorna watched Stump as he sat on the stool next to the Goat Man. "Go bug Stump, ask him for a date or sumpthin."

Peggy didn't want to bother him, but she feared getting Lorna angry more than she feared upsetting Stump. She approached the bar feeling the tension coming from Stump the closer she came. At the end of the bar she stopped. Alfred had pivoted towards her on his stool, and with wary eyes confronted her uncertainty.

"Yer awfully pretty tonight darlin. Lookin for a little company?"

"I just come up to talk to Stump, not you."

"What cha want with Stump, my friend is uh man of few words, specially when it comes to the weaker sex."

"Like I said, I don't want nothin from you. Just wanted to say hi to him an stuff."

Stump was frightened and had turned towards the street. He wished his food was here and that she wasn't. He thought back to the safety of the old barn and the security of the woods.

"You don't wanna talk to Stump. You don't even wanna be up here. He's same as you, cept you got sumpthin they want, least now they do, when that's gone you'll be bout as welcome as he is. Why don'tcha go back to yer game an let him eat in peace."

Lorna sensing her plan falling apart called to her friend, "Not him Peg, the retard, he's uh nut it's no fun messin with him."

Alfred pivoted quickly towards Lorna, "You bet yer big ass I'm nuts, but yer ugly, at least I might have some lucid moments to look forward to."

Leo laughed. The two old women were silent, mentally recording their versions of what was being said, for after church discussions. Lorna made an obscene gesture in the direction of the bar.

"I swear this town's so busy shittin on people they must put Exlax in the water tower. Can't wait till we get the fuck outta here."

Peggy laughed at her friend's joke and nodded her head in agreement to leaving town. It was their dream; jobs and an apartment in Saint Cloud, maybe even The Cities, night school for secretary until the baby. Things were going to be better. She laughed a lot, but hadn't really found much that was funny, in a good way, so far in her life. Lorna was the only person that could abide her clinging nature. Her mother disapproved but Peggy feared the loneliness she knew, more than the reputation her mother warned might rub off onto her by associating with Lorna. They looked old and tired. For all their youth they were the old ladies in the booth; husbands unmet instead of dead, but waiting on time, for moments to pass, lines to be said and forgotten. Their existence would be long but not full. The things they had counted on being worth waiting for would prove to be nothing. It wasn't in them for their lives to be remembered much beyond their passing. Some day they would dig out yellowing photos taken in times they had wished away, and say "wasn't I sumpthin back then." Not much longer after that someone would look at the same picture and say, "now who could this have been," "damned if I know maybe yer Gramma or her mother," and then pull it from an album of other forgotten "stuff", and put it in a box to use it's spot for pictures of things yet remembered.

Alfred turned to Stump who still sat stiffly studying an auction flyer he couldn't read. "How bout loanin me uh couple bucks."

"Ain't got none." Stump's hand had slipped down and was pressed hard against the right pocket of his trousers. With that move Alfred knew not only that his friend was lying, but was also certain that with time, and a little effort, he could get him to part with at least enough for a bottle of White Port.

Leo sat a bowl of steaming soup in front of Stump and turned to the grill where a burger sizzled in a pool of steaming grease.

"You said all the soup was gone cept a bowl you was savin for yerself. What is this shit, yuh like Stump better'n me."

"Yeah. But that ain't the reason he gets the soup. Ellen sets it aside when we get low cuz she knows it's his favrit, but like I said I do like him lots better'n you."

Alfred didn't appear totally surprised or hurt by this seemingly painful admission. "God I'm hungry Stump, I can't even remember the last time I ate." He rubbed his oddly protruding stomach, and looked at his companion with sadly drooping eyes. "Yep uh plate uh food sure would set nice just now."

"Ray said yuh gets more money en me, an if I give yuh some, yuh just get drunk."

"Goverment men don't know nuthin, young pup, he wasn't there, Korea, Christ it was cold. Some damn welfare worker gonna tell me how to spend what they owes me."

Alfred had served during Korea, though the nearest he'd gotten to combat had been The Clammer Bar in Lakehurst New Jersey, where he was learning to pack parachutes. A marine that didn't appreciate Alfred's ability at finding sensitive spots in others, had pummeled his head with a pair of beefy fists. After release from sick bay Alfred had finished his training and been assigned to an aircraft carrier. Things were never quite the same for him again, whether it was the blows to his head, or a chemical imbalance that would have come along to torment him eventually regardless of the abuses his body would suffer. He argued with people even when alone, and laughed mysteriously at inappropriate times. He was granted a medical discharge, and sent home with a small disability pension, which provided him the money to slowly poison himself with alcohol. Heavy drinking was the only area of Navy training which he had shown any real interest in, or aptitude for. He often bragged that if he could have stayed in he would have ended up an admiral.

"Tell yuh what if yuh give me uh buck, I'll get uh bottle an meet yuh under the loading ramp."

Stump surrendered the dollar and watched Alfred slip out the door. He didn't know for sure that Alfred had no intention of meeting him later, and it didn't matter. Stump wasn't going to go looking for him. Sharing a bottle with Alfred was more unpleasant than having him work him for money, and a dollar was a small price to pay for silence.

Stump studied reflections on the dark window pane. The colored bar lights made it seem cheerful in the little tavern. Using the last scrap of bun from his hamburger sandwich, he mopped the bowl for a film of potato soup, which somehow had escaped his scraping spoon. He drank a second beer, savoring this one, drinking slowly, and watching the girls play pool when he could.

Leo was busy behind the bar twisting on the hose coupling for a keg. He pulled the empty barrel out of the cooler with an empty clunk, grabbed it by the side, paused reconsidering and then looked at Stump. "Yuh wanna help me here for uh minute?"

Stump grinned, slid off his stool, walked behind the bar, and easily lifted the empty keg to his shoulder. As he followed Leo to the back room they passed the pool table, he glanced shyly at the Slayton girl. She looked back at him, briefly meeting his eyes and then looking away and towards Lorna to see if she had witnessed the compassion that had passed between them.

Alfred had hit pay dirt with his remark about Peggy being like Stump. Though she would have scored higher on an intelligence test, and had at least been tolerated in high school until dropping out, she knew, had sensed from teachers, and heard from friends and stepfather, that nearly everyone else was smarter than she was. This was the first time however that anyone had ever compared her to Stump. She added it to a long list of things she had to worry about.

A naked bulb lighted the back room from its perch in the bare rafters. Rows of kegs both empty and full stood on the cold cement floor. Soda bottles in their wooden crates and cardboard beer cases stacked chest high formed aisles leading into the darkness that existed beyond the dusty circle of light. Leo pointed at a sixteen gallon barrel of Schmidt's. Stump sat the empty keg down, and picked up the full one, clutching it to his chest. They walked back into the bar, as the bulb flicked off, leaving the room in blackness. In the corner a rat returned to it's gnawing at the sulfur laced bread Leo had left for it earlier in the day, in the alley behind a dog tipped over a garbage can with a loud metallic clang, and started feasting on the fish entrails left there the day before by Stump.

Stump studiously ignored the girls as he trailed behind Leo on the way back to the front of the bar. He pushed the keg into the slot left vacant by its predecessor and walked back to his stool to watch the reconnection of lines.

"Spose yuh figger yuh gotta free beer comin."

Stump's grin was Leo's answer. Leo sat a mug of suds, with just a bit of amber liquid in the bottom, in front of Stump, and then returned to his game of solitaire.

Stump looked out the window watching the street and reflections from inside, as always feeling somehow separate from either. Both sides of the window felt the same. It was coated with fog. The moist bar air touched a window cold from the northwest wind, and vapor turned to moisture. His face and the lights from the beer signs were blurred, making both more beautiful, soft like an old time photograph, the colors unreal. Where enough condensation gathered, it beaded up, and the tears streaked down in erratic jagged spurts.

A car drove by outside sending spray from puddles up onto the sidewalk. Hurrying in the gentle rain, a cat ran across the street lugging the disembodied head of a fish. Ice was already forming in the tree branches high up where the waning warmth of the earth had no power. Like an ancient knight slowly wrapped in layers of cold armor by a demented page, each twig was being coated with a weight that the limb couldn't hold.

Stump left when the group of out of town hunters from earlier in the day returned and started playing pool with Lorna and Peggy. The laughter and jokes were good at times but tonight they made him feel lonely. He stood under the arched doorway of the VFW, trying to decide what next to do to avoid returning to his room. A shadowy shape darted out from beneath a car parked on the other side of the street, and joined him under the dry roof. It rubbed back and forth on his legs, purring noisily, demanding his attention. He crouched and rubbed the little gray cat's ears. The cat in turn sat down and began licking whitefish slime from its whiskers.

"Where was yuh Stumpy, waited there for uh long time, an when yuh dint show I got kind uh worried, so I came lookin for yuh." Alfred stood before him staggering, and pumping out a mist of wine smelling breath. He reached down and pulled on the nylon fish stringer which kept his much too large trousers at odds with gravity, a part of his daily routine, more frequent, but as regular, as the coughing fits that left bits of his interior lying around on the sidewalks of town.

"Yuh thought I was gonna stiff yuh on the wine dint yuh? Well yuh was wrong! I got it right here." He reached inside the old suit coat and pulled out a nearly empty bottle of White Port and held it hesitantly out to his friend.

Stump shook his head in refusal. "I ready had as many as Ray say's is ok."

"Yuh see Ray here, hell no! Just yer ole bud, now come on, it's half yer's yuh know."

Stump took the offered bottle and tilted it back. Even in the dim light of the entryway he could see tiny flecks of suspended matter dance in what wine remained. He thought of the results from Alfred's coughing and handed the bottle back.

"There's things floatin round in there."

Alfred shrugged and finished off the bottle, wiped his mouth with the grimy suit coat sleeve, and stood the empty up in the corner of the small enclosure, label out, lined up with a knot hole the shape of a prostrate rooster. He stood briefly straight and saluted it with more energy than he had mustered during his entire episode in uniform.

"Yuh got any more uh the money Leo gave yuh? Cuz I got thirty six cents. We could get another bottle. Damn shame yuh din't come lookin for me when yuh said yuh would."

"I spent most uh it on smokes, Ray showed me how its lots cheaper to buy em by the carton an not run out all uh time."

"Well that just shows how much he knows, cuz here yuh are spent out on smokes, an me dyin uh thirst. Yuh gotta realize yuh can only smoke em one at uh time, an if yer all invested in smokes, yuh might haf'ta pass up on other opportunities. Christ Stump, don't lissen to that kid so much, he ain't lookin out for yer intrests like I am."

The car that had passed by earlier came around the end of the block again, passed beyond the entryway, stopped and backed up to their shelter.

Alfred stiffened into a menacing "what do you want" fists to his side's position and then relaxed. "I know them kids, looks like opportunities gonna knock for me tonight after all."

The passenger side window rolled down as Alfred approached the vehicle. "Hey Goatman Yuh wanna make uh buck?"

"Depends, what I gotta do?"

"Get uh case uh malt liquor an uh quart uh Jim Beam for us."

"Jeeze that's illegal must be worth more'n uh buck for uh feller to risk that kind uh trouble."

"Look all we got is uh buck extra next time we'll make it right."

"Well shit, you boys been good customers, I spose this once I could help yuh out, but don't forget bout next time. Gimme the damn money, an meet me over in the alley back uh the liquor store, in bout ten minutes."

The passenger side boy extended a handful of bills. "Don't fuck us over Goat Man or we'll do some serious ass kickin."

Alfred gave the youth a contemptuous look, "Yuh got me shittin all over my self, shouldn't be scarin yer only connection to the good stuff that way."

He took the offered bills and stepped back into the entryway with Stump as the car drove away.

"Yuh wanna come with me, not into the store, but just with me, yuh can share the bottle I get outta my cut."

Stump didn't have any pressing plans and shook his head in agreement.

They walked the darkened side streets to the municipal liquor store. Stump stood back in the shadows while Alfred went in to make the purchases. He was soon back out in the dark with Stump. A flat box full of cans and a paper sack that appeared to have a bottle inside sat on the ground at his feet. The car full of teenagers entered the alley and stopped slightly ahead of where they stood. Alfred picked up the illegal beverages and walked out into the dim light. He carried them to the open window and handed them through to the eager boy in the front passenger seat.

"What is this shit we asked for malt liqour an yuh get this fuckin Cold Springs cheapest damn beer in the world. Give us some money back or yer gonna wish yuh had."

Stump stepped slightly out of the shadows, not as an intended threat, but to hear better what was going on. One of the boys in the rear of the car called the sudden and unexpected arrival of a third party to the others attention.

"Who the fuck yuh got with yuh?"

"None uh yer damn business who I got, yuh got yer booze an I got more'n the lousy buck yuh was gonna gimme. That damn malt licker tastes like piss anyway, an if yuh don't like how I do business go to the cops an complain to them."

"Why don't yuh go back to the woods an fuck yer goats agin yuh crazy bastard."

"I only did that once, an when you was born I figgered God was punishin me for my sin, an I didn't do it no more."

The car sped down the alley with arms sticking out the windows extending single defiant fingers. Alfred snickered, "little pricks think they're gonna stick it to me."

"Them boys are gonna hurt yuh some day."

"Nea, they ain't even got uniforms, to really hurt somebody yuh gotta have a uniform. If yuh wanna bomb somebody's house, or lock em up, an shoot em full uh poison, yuh just gotta be wearin uh uniform. Those little shit heads need me a hell of uh lot more'n I need them."

"I'm goin home. I ain't thirsty no more."

"Shit Stump don't worry bout them punks. Lets go have some wine, I'll even get yuh yer own bottle."

"Nope I'm sleepy." He opened his mouth in an exaggerated yawn, and then wandered down the alley towards the old hotel.

In the lobby a group of the old men waiting out the nursing home, or death, were sitting in front of the television set, on couches and chairs which showed their years as clearly as the men, or the building they shared. Somewhere far away two black men were boxing in front of a camera to the hoots and hollering of soft bodied men who filled the air with smoke and barbaric noise. The crowd that sat in the arena and the people with eyes fixed on flickering TV's tried to steal the strength and youth of the young men as they maimed each other. For a short time they felt invincible shouting advice to unhearing ears, demonstrating with clumsy jabs, and punches, how they would deal with an opponent. Feeling a sense of victory when their favorite dealt the defeating blow to someone they had never seen, but suddenly, and for a short time hated enough to wish harm on.

Stump passed by unnoticed, ascended the stairs, walked down the hall and into his room. He sat on the edge of his bed, looking out the window, watching the reflections of lights on the wet streets.

Chapter 12

Sunday morning at the Anderman house was a painful, slow awakening, where simple requests, and instructions, became a Babel of sounds, in long dead, or unintelligible dialects, that left the listener in an apparent state of confusion. The children hated church. They were pried from warm beds, forced into their good clothes, and reminded constantly not to make a mess of them until they were safely put back in the closet and comfortable weekend pants and shirts put back on. Knowing that they couldn't have breakfast until after Mass (from fear of contaminating the stomach before accepting the body of Christ, which came every month to the Post Office in a shipment from the Bishop in Crookston), didn't speed their ascending. This month's supply of hosts had arrived only the Tuesday before in the same truck that had brought the Christmas Wish books from Sears Roebuck.

The children made excuses and moved slowly, hoping that if they were tardy enough their mother would cancel the day's worship to avoid the embarrassment of a late arrival. Where this misguided belief came from was a mystery, occasionally they were spared the drone of the rosary, or on an especially slow morning even choir practice, but they were always in their pew in time to stand while the priest made his stellar entrance. The cleric firmly enthroned, the parishioners could briefly follow his lead and sit.

The older boys looked up and down the rows of pews with something less then pious interest, nodding in agreement or elbowing when it seemed the other was missing the entrance of a girl worth looking at.

Fred and Philip sat together in apparent agony, choking on tight collars, and the odor of the perfumes, colognes and powders that wafted off the worshipers. Church was a little more bearable with padded kneelers and the Mass performed in English. The Latin had been pretty, and mysterious, but now there was some meaning in the midst of all the ceremony.

Fred's favorite diversion in church was trying to get Philip to laugh, something that normally didn't prove to be a very difficult task. In the company of so many adults, and under the sad watchful eyes of the holy statues, it took all of his imagination to find the one thing that even the lip biting technique of his younger brother couldn't withstand. This morning Mrs. Williams sat directly in front of Fred. A stern looking woman with a mink stole. The gift of a long dead husband, the fur wasn't a well made garment, and had suffered through many summers of storage. The heads of the little creatures had glass eyes, beads actually that stared out from poorly tanned stiff heads, the mouths clamping down on tails, held the balding hides in place on her skinny shoulders. Fred turned towards Philip, making sure he was unobserved by his mother, he crossed his eyes in a vain attempt at mimicking the vacant stare of the mink. Philip obviously found the result humorous, but choked back his laughter, and looked to the ever patient Joseph for comfort. Fred waited, knowing that his goal would be accomplished well before communion, and that that was the only time his younger brother had a chance of putting family members between him and his tormentor. Curiosity finally overcame Philip and he glanced towards his brother. The ever vigilant Fred, seeing a chance, stuck his finger in the partly opened mouth of the dead animal, let out a short yelp of real pain, and withdrew a finger that had a small drop of blood on it. The clasp, as defunct as the rest of the antique fur piece, had been assisted for years by a short straight pin that pierced the ear and mink's tail, and lay concealed in between the two, to be discovered by Fred's exploring finger. Philip exploded in laughter, and was joined by several adults that had been enjoying Fred's efforts, from the pew behind. Mrs. Williams turned slightly in response to the spasm of life that had caused her mink to stir seemingly on its own for the first time since the advent of internal combustion.

Mr. Anderman grabbed Philip by the forearm and nodded to the back of the church. By the sidewalk all signs of merriment had disappeared from Philip's face.

"What the heck was that all about?"

Philip, following the code, had a brief, dishonest answer, "Nothin".

"Yuh start laughing in church an it's nothin?"

He would have pressed the interrogation but the organ inside announced the entrance of their religious leader. Back inside, Philip was separated from Fred by his father, who suspected the true cause of the explosion of humor. Both boys sat through the remainder of the service for the first time dreading its inevitable end.

Up and down they went in careful pantomime of each other, standing, sitting, kneeling, and standing again. But always a respectful pause behind the priest when the infrequent chances to sit came. Brought together for a variety of reasons under a shared roof of worship, people examined their lives, their neighbors, looked for meaning to their existence, and occasionally even prayed.

After church the young people hurried outside and stood by the steps, talking to friends, and waiting for parents to finish doing the same inside. The boys and men with hands tucked deep in pockets for warmth and security talked of weather, hunting, work, or sports. The girls and women examined each other and maliciously made casual remarks about those absent, late, or at least safely out of range of their well meant words. The children looked at the trees, and the miracle of sun light shining through a million ice crystals as it passed out of the prisms on each hanging twig, and descended to earth.

The streets were wet. People who lived near the church hurried home, with their eyes alert to passing motorists, and the spray that came from their tires. Everyone seemed happy. This could have been because of a shared feeling of forgiven sin, or because of an escape from the confines of merciless pews. The resulting joy from either of these, or the combination of both, made time spent in spiritual bondage seem a good exchange, at least until the next Sunday, when the demand was made again.

The car ride home for the Anderman's was usually fun. The three older boys in the back, and Philip wedged between his parents, in the front. He would turn, and point, and jabber about things of interest to only him, and not be shushed. The common feeling being that his normal silence during the course of the Mass was bound to result in an explosion of sound after his release. Both he and Fred were subdued today, waiting the unavoidable questions, and working out plausible excuses for the complete breach of etiquette.

"You boys gonna have to be separated like we used to, or are yuh old enough to be in public together without causing embarrassment."

"Any boy that can't leave his brother alone in Church is too darn immature to take hunting."

Fred looked down at his injured finger and absorbed the lesson from his fathers warning. He had been looking forward to the first year he could tag along deer hunting, the first year he would be allowed to carry a gun, harassing Philip wasn't worth losing that privilege.

Mrs. Anderman looked across at her husband. It seemed that when the boys reached Fred's age they couldn't be coerced into doing things by her appealing to their concern for her feelings. Motivation seemed to come either from the company and approval of their father, or threats of losing access to their friends. She hated appealing to her husband for interventions in matters that were once easily handled through her authority alone. It seemed that he usually waited for the request or at least only acted when the behavior was too obnoxious to be ignored.

As they passed the Lake Shore Hotel, Philip saw Stump standing on the sidewalk looking up into the trees at the ice. "What's he do for a livin Dad?"

"Oh nothin much, gets welfare money I spose, does odd jobs, strong as a damn bull, worked side by side with ole Emil out to the farm till he died. You ain't been bothering him have yuh, he's got enough problems without a bunch uh kids pickin on him."

"I saw him hide back in the woods yesterday when we went in for the first load uh hay out to the Anson place," Tom added from the rear seat.

"He still goes out there? Surprised he'd even remember how to find it. That was where he grew up. See that's the old Jenson place. You wouldn't remember Tom, John probly would, but you couldn't have been more than five or six. We used to go out there an borrow uh tool once in uh while, an I used to bring the tractor over an help out when his would break down, but like I say yuh were perty young."

"He'd take us up in the hay mow to show us where the cat hid her kittens. I didn't know it was him, but I remember even then thinkin it was weird, uh grown up playin hide an seek, an bein so happy when we'd show up."

"I'll bet he don't even got to go to church. If he don't go to church won't he end up in hell?" Fred had been preoccupied with damnation for several months. He felt sure that hell would have to be awful to come close to the wraths that ran rampant through his dreams; women that changed in the middle of their nocturnal visitations to other things, unspeakable things, which left him even more frightened and confused about what was happening to his brain and body.

The sun warmed the wires crisscrossing the streets overhead enough for them to be freed of their loads of ice. It smashed down in long strips leaving the occupants of cars laughing with relief after passing through the noisy bombardments unscathed.

Frank looked out the window as they passed the Richardson house. Patti was rushing her younger sister away from their car as her family returned from church. With perfect timing, she turned towards the street as the Anderman's drove by, and waved. Frank nodded casually and then throwing caution to the wind smiled warmly and waved back.

Fred and Tom started making smooching noises, hugged, and Fred whispered a poor imitation of Frank, "Oh Patti I wuv you." They both laughed at their brother's discomfort. Philip looked over the edge of the front seat and joined the torment by grotesquely puckering up his lips. Their smiling parents remained silent.

At home the boys followed their father to Tom's Hudson, and watched Tom open the hood. The motor lay there beneath layers of caked grease, oil, and dirty spark plug wires. Tom had used part of his pay from Anson to buy a used water pump from Bert's Junkyard. Bert's guarantee was that "if that one don't work, take one off the one next to it, an maybe ya'll get lucky."

"Get away from that greasy monstrosity, any spots on them clothes an I'll line yuh all up an start paddlin. Yer father will be first." Mrs. Anderman took a playful swat at her husband's backside and herded the group away from the car and into the house.

Everyone went to their rooms and put away the vestiges of Sunday sobriety, and came back down to breakfast, and to go their separate ways.

Chapter 13

Down in the swamp by the creek Philip, Tim, and Anne sat on old tire rims. The tall spruce which grew on the only high spot in the marsh towered above them. Sheltered from the eyes of passers by they had a small fire going. They played a gruesome game, pushing a plastic soldier's body into the fire, and retrieving it, just prior to combustion. The torched appendages could then be twisted to new and interesting angles. Charred weapons pointed behind or at the figurines helmeted head. They had played at war a while but had grown tired of it. Experimenting with fire, and its wonderful effect on the green plastic miniatures, had proved to be much more interesting. Their fire was made of dead twigs, and cattail stocks, the little smoke it created was lost in the green bows above them.

All three had wet shoes and socks, the mud washed off in the forgiving creek. Wet shoes in a world full of mud puddles couldn't be traced to the swamp so the children were relaxed. They had examined Stump's spot in the milkweeds, and hadn't found anything of value. The cat Stump had thrown into the swamp created a stir, but later Tim admitted that he had seen it laying dead by the tracks on Friday morning. Philip, still not convinced of accidental death, pointed out that the cat's head was twisted around, and reminded them all of what Deak Johnson had once said about what he had seen Stump do to cats. Anne restated her low opinion of Mr. Johnson and any stories he was even involved in. They gave the cat a sailor's funeral, a rock tied to its hind legs with a short length of wire. It now lay in a back water hole, patchy yellow fur, mingling with decayed vegetation, in a common grave. Anne insisted that they sing Amazing Grace, but ended the lamenting when she realized that she alone knew the right words.

Philip looked up from the damage inflicted on a rifleman during his last test of fire. He used his index finger to adjust the position of the slightly drooping gun barrel. The plastic burned initially and continued to burn even after his finger was securely in his mouth. "damn it to heck", he mumbled around his blistering digit.

"Umm! You gonna go to hell for takin the Lord's name in vane on a Sunday," Anne piously rebuffed.

"I never, just said damn is all, sides I forgot it was Sunday."

"Still yuh gotta confess that one."

"Spose I should say just what I said, or tell em I disobeyed my parents."

"Yer folks ever tell yuh not to say bad words on Sunday?"

"I'm not sposed to say em at all, ain't sposed to play with matches either."

All three looked at the fire and considered their crime. Anne decided that absolution would be best sought through a plea of general disobedience to parents, which would include, even if in omission, all sins committed on this day.

The sun started to change the trees into long shadows that lay flat on the ground, pointing out towards the creek. A cold breeze came over the bank causing the branches to rub together above their heads. The shadows moved accordingly. Birds flew to the shelter of the pines and roosted in the thick cover of needles. The children heaped sand on the little fire, and packed more dirt against the side of the log, which had refused to burn. When the flames had been smothered they packed their army in a Folgers can and left.

A wisp of smoke peeked out from the corner of the log it was grabbed by the breeze and carried away. The children's fire had eaten away into its center. In the punky, rotting heart, the fire had found dry fuel. Drawing air from the cracks on the log's ends it could smolder for hours. If the wind brought more rain the flames would be extinguished. No rain came, only a dry cold wind that blew through the long night.

Fred and Philip started out together the next morning for school. Before they reached the railroad tracks above the swamp they could see the black charred stalks of the cattails and smell the acrid odor of burnt marsh grass. The creek had kept fire from reaching the buildings that bordered the swamp. The lower limbs of the pines had been scorched, but the trees would survive. Brush that grew beside the stream in several places had lost bark, and would have to start over from the roots, so in spite of the devastating appearances, the actual damage from the fire was slight.

Philip was afraid, and for the first time, he felt how truly bad a day could become so soon after breakfast. Playing in the swamp and all the things he had done wrong in his short life were insignificant in comparison to this. Playing with fire was what burned families up, or caused forest fires. People went to prison, and children to reform school, for starting fires. The creek had saved him, as it had saved the Bank, and the other buildings. He knew he would have to talk to Anne and Tim, and decide on a story to tell, if they needed one. He hoped no one had seen them playing in the swamp.

"I think I see Anne and Tim comin, I'm gonna wait an walk with them."

"Yuh look kind uh sick. Maybe yuh otta go home an have Ma take yer temperature. I'd get outta school if I looked like that."

Philip was unsure of how to take the last comment, but let it pass unchallenged. "Nea like I say I'm gonna walk with them."

Fred shrugged his shoulders and walked away alone. His steps causing swirls of soot, and charred grass, to rise up from their hard ground resting place, fly about in the crisp morning air and gently sit back on earth as he passed.

Philip sat down on the icy steel rail. The cold metal was uncomfortable, but he rested there, hands cupping chin, elbows braced on knees, looking out on the ruin he had caused. The blackbirds were gone, the creek channel and backwaters bare of their cattail cover, reflected a hard unforgiving blue sky.

He was so engrossed in self torture, and "if only's", Philip didn't even look up to watch the approach of his friends.

"We saw it glowin in the night, fire trucks an everything, Dad got a call bout two-thirty this mornin, an he's been gone ever since."

Mr. Petersen was a volunteer fireman, a source of pride to both of his children. This morning they weren't bragging.

"You didn't tell did yuh? You didn't tell em bout the fire?" Philip's question had the whine of a plea to it.

"Are you crazy, coarse we didn't tell! We keep our mouths shut. Nobody knows nothin, an we keep it that way. Dad called Ma when they got it out to tell her he wouldn't be home for uh while. He said they figger ole Stump started it cuz he's all the time down there smokin. If any body gets in trouble it'll be him. Hell he might a started it anyway. I know we put ours out. Probly was him."

The boys looked at Anne with no real conviction but nodded their heads in unison to her line of reasoning.

Philip stood, and the trio walked towards school, creating their own whirlwinds of ash with each footfall.

Chapter 14

Stump stood by the fire station garage doors watching the men roll up and straighten hoses. They were laughing and calling him an old pyromaniac. Not knowing what he was being accused of he laughed with them. Three children ignoring the interesting activity and the chance to chant a "Stump in the Dump" ditty crossed the street and hurried by.

Emma Schwartz looked over the edge of her half glasses and out the dust smudged window. Down in the street below Stump watched as the fire truck backed into the garage stall.

"He's a damned nuisance, that's what he is, a nuisance and a danger as long as he's allowed to walk these streets unsupervised. Something's gonna have to be done with him before he ends up hurtin somebody. On purpose or not, won't make any difference either way. Damage will be done an then they'll do sumpthin, too late, but they'll do sumpthin then."

She turned from her window and walked past the volunteer fireman's desk where Charlie Petersen was busy scratching out a brief report in a ledger book. She pushed open a large door and stepped out on the front step.

"Stump you better be careful with them darned cigarettes uh yours. Yuh got lucky this time, next time property might get destroyed, or somebody hurt, then there'll be hell to pay. They'll slam yuh back in the loony bin faster'n yuh can blink an eye. I'm tellin yuh this cuz your mother was a dear friend uh mine, an though the pain an disappointment she felt when you were born was almost too much for her to stand, she still tried to bring you up right. I tell yuh this just like I know she would a wanted me to. You quit causin trouble! You come from a good family, hard workers everyone of em. Just cuz you're feeble minded is no excuse, people won't put up with yuh if yuh do bad things. Now get goin, go do sumpthin constructive for a change."

Charlie Petersen closed the log book. "You were a little hard on him Emma. Ain't no proof he started it. Could uh been uh lotta things, even a cigarette tossed from the train would a done it. Even if he did do it, it didn't hurt nothin. Hell we burn it off ourselves just for practice every spring. Coarse it ain't at two in the mornin, with a northwest wind blowin, but like I say ain't no proof he done it, an nobody ever complained about him bein careless with fire before."

Emma glared at Charlie, but said nothing, and returned to her watching post. She sat down, folded her arms across her stomach, leaned slightly back in the chair, and began selectively ignoring what went on behind her in the office, as she studied the town.

Chapter 15

Stump entered the alley, which divided the respectable Down Town stores and offices, from the Lake Shore Hotel and the other businesses that faced the railroad tracks. Coming from the other end of the alley he saw his Social Worker, Ray approach. They met at the rear of the hotel where a set of rickety, weathered, wooden steps satisfied the State Fire Marshall's rules.

"Hi there Carl! Gosh its good to see you." Ray extended his hand and firmly shook Stump's weakly placed paw.

Stump knew after the first year of working with Ray, and after the rescue from the state hospital, that Ray was happy to see him, and wasn't a "glad hander" mouthing insincerities, but he still felt uncomfortable around that much warmth.

"I'm not here to bug you today. Just checkin in on Alfred. Yuh wouldn't know if he's in would yuh?"

Stump felt a bit of relief, not that he minded Ray's visits, but after his lecture from "the one who always watches, Emma," he didn't feel like discussing something he knew wasn't his fault. This also explained Ray's foot approach and rear entry up the, fire escape. Alfred was always avoiding Ray, and would sneak out, and down these hazardous steps when ever he heard the sputtering exhaust of Ray's Corvaire approach the hotel. With the increasing popularity of the sound-alike Volkswagen, Alfred was constantly climbing down the steps, or ducking behind buildings, to postpone discussions on the benefits of Thorazine and Lithium, or the dangers of drinking.

"Say did'ja happen to see that fire last night? Wow! That was a close one. The wind just about took it down town." Ray's question, and statement, were delivered in an easy going by the way manner, but his eyes were doing a very careful study of Stump, for any signs of nervousness, or avoidance. "Have yuh heard how it got started?"

"Emma Schwartz says I done it, an I gotta go back to the loony bin if I don't start behavin, but I never done it."

"Do yuh know anything at all bout how it might of started?"

Stump looked at the ground as if there was something that concerned him more down around the oddly taped up toe of his shoe. "Nope." He nervously scraped at the toe of one boot with the other. "Whatcha wanna see Alfred for?"

"Oh just need to talk to him is all. I better get up there before he goes out for his morning constitutional. See yuh later Carl. Don't do anything I wouldn't do."

Ray tested the banister with a stiff shake of his hand, shook his head in disbelief and started a pensive climb up the narrow steep treads. He was confident that Stump hadn't started the fire but was totally unconvinced of his ignorance about the fire's origin.

Stump continued on his way down the garbage strewn alley. Eddie Eikilson saw him enter his grocery store and hurried up to Stump with hand extended, leaving a case of pork and beans mid aisle and un-priced.

With a firm, insincere grasp, Stump was greeted. "Say, just the feller I been waitin to see. My friend how'd yuh like to make a couple dollars. No! Don'tcha say uh word uh thanks. Like I always say, if yuh can't help out them that's less fortunate what's the point uh havin anything. Now I got uh couple cords uh wood comin in tomorrow and I'll give yuh two bucks to throw it down my window well an then go down an stack it up nice an neat. My wife'll be there to show yuh where to stack it an open the window for yuh."

Stump was tempted to ask for more, the way Will had shown him to, to get more for cleaning fish, but remembered other jobs at Eikilson's, and agreed to the price. Mrs. Eikilson was a nice lady, who drank, and if he showed up in the early afternoon, after she had drank a bit, but before she had drunk too much, she would give him a huge lunch and slip him a few extra dollars, "for being such a nice boy".

Stump bought two palm sized cherry pies and walked out onto the street with his tiny grocery bag firmly clasped in his hand. A large grain truck came down the street, carrying wheat, and with dirty frozen snow still sticking to its sides, from a storm in the Dakotas. It slowed as it passed the corner where the town cop usually parked, and waited for speeders. Then the driver shifted gears again, and roared out of town, headed for Duluth. Stump scratched his ear and looked down the street, first east and then west, the huge grain hauler was the only vehicle on the road in either direction. There were some men pouring cement down by the lawyer's office. A lady had tripped on an uneven crack in the sidewalk and was suing. She had to go all the way to Bemidji to find a lawyer to represent her.

Stump wandered down the street stopping to look at various activities or to look in windows. He saw a huge woman, and her stringy husband, load a brand new Frigidaire freezer into the back of a blue pickup truck. He would have helped, but if anything bad happened he was afraid of being blamed, so instead he stood and watched. They grunted and shoved the stores two wheeled cart up the sagging planks. It was a monumental feat, and well worth the watching. The small man stood in the bed of the truck pulling. The veins of his arm's bulging, his wife pushed from the ground, her body threatening the structural integrity of the faded print dress, which under normal conditions barely sheathed her. The freezer reached the top of the planking, and bumped down into the pickup, just as Harry Eikilson reached the street to offer help. The man shook his head in refusal and disgust. His wife climbed into the loaded down truck, combining her weight with that of the appliance, and causing the springs to sag. The man hopped down and flopped the cart down onto the sidewalk by Harry. He walked silently around the front of his lopsided truck, climbed in the driver's seat, and followed the grain truck out of town. Harry grabbed the cart and pushed it back into the hardware store his father had bought him.

Stump stood on the edge of the street watching as the workers troweled the surface of the lawyer's cement. They rubbed it and polished until the rocks were all buried beneath a smooth slowly hardening cap, and then they took a stiff broom and marred the walkway to save the attorney from future problems. Their employer stood in front of his window peering out at the men working; his neat gray suit a contrast to the cement splattered work pants and shirts of those who toiled in front of him. He was paying them and wanted to make sure that they earned it.

A frolicsome Labrador rushed around the corner, its long red tongue hanging down in a friendly manner. Spotting the men, and deciding to investigate, it ducked under the saw horse, and happily ran out into the uncured cement. The men swore at him and chased him away. It's thick black tail was still wagging, undeterred by his less than cordial welcome, as he rounded Fifth Street at Stump's heels. They walked down the hill to the city dock, and Stump roughed the appreciative dogs head and ears, as he instructed it about the importance of staying out of trouble.

The launches had all been pulled out of the water, and were stored in a distant field, stacked in their cradles with heavy tarpaulins drawn down and tied around them to keep out the snow and ice of winter. A few duck boats were still tied to slips, but the docking area was quite deserted. Stump sat on a low piling, and ate his pies, occasionally sharing a bit of crust with the ever observant dog. When he finished eating, he smoked a cigarette. The smoke slipped over his shoulder, and was gently swept away in the Northwest wind. The water sparkled like a billion diamonds, as it danced in the light breeze, ring billed gulls spun above his head, and begged for pie. He finished his cigarette, and offered the butt up to the birds with a flip of his fingers. The nearest one took it in a speedy dive, carried it briefly, and dropped it, for another to make a pass at, before it hissed into the lake. Stump laughed and idly petted his companion's smooth black coat. Across the bay a raft of ducks jumped up, and stretched their wings, in a short flight from one bed of wild rice to another. From the dock they were just a moving black smudge over the lake's blue surface.

Stump picked up a piece of drift wood and tossed it into the cold water. The Labrador dove into the water and swam smoothly out to the stick and then brought it back in to shore. He threw it again and the dog repeated the retrieve. They played fetch until the noon whistle gave them both a much needed break. At the VFW club they parted company, Stump going for lunch, and Charlie the dog to see if the men replacing the lawyer's sidewalk were interested in playing some more.

A few regulars were sipping beers, waiting while their burgers sizzled on the grill. Stump nodded at Leo and took the furthest back booth. Some of the customers stared inquisitively at him, he got nervous and his index finger took an experimental probe into his nostril, the people turned away and rejoined conversations about the nights blaze.

The construction crew came in and ordered lunch. Leo brought them a round of beers.

"You fellers stickin it to Larson perty good I hope."

"Hell Leo, four an hour, but it ain't worth it. He keeps uh askin dumb assed questions, an wonderin if maybe we otta do it this way, or that way. We'd uh been done an hour ago if he'd uh stayed at his desk an let us work. All the attention he's payin to us yuh'd think we made as much as he does. He even asked us to fix a chunk of curb that's breakin up. I told him we'd haf'ta form it up an it'd cost more. He had the nerve to call us uh bunch uh crooks, said we could just slop it in an pad it into shape. I told him, "for Christ sake we ain't makin mud pies here," then he says when he went to college he did some construction work an they use'ta do it like that all the time. I told him, "I don't know what kind uh outfit you worked for but we don't do business like that. He took off then an told us to clean the spatters off his windows. Since we got the job by the hour we put Steve on it, must uh took him twenty minutes." Steve made an obscene gesture at the foreman but joined in the laughter.

As the group at the bar talked Stump finished his lunch. He slid the empty mug back and forth between his well scraped plate and the napkin dispenser, hoping that Leo or Ellen would see the signal, and ask if he wanted another beer. Both could obviously see him, but didn't respond to his suggestion. Stump got up, and was attempting to leave the bar, when the door pushed open in front of him, and a denim encrusted teenager swaggered in, followed closely by two similarly clad boys.

"Jesus Key-riste if it ain't the feeb fire bug that tried burnin the fuckin town down." He paused, waiting for laughter, his friends obliged from behind, but the bar crowd was silent. "Would uh been the best damn thing that ever happened round here. Too bad he didn't start it up in that damn hotel, would uh cleared some room to put up uh decent place to eat." Once again he was rewarded by the dutiful heehaws of his entourage, and silence from the bar.

The regulars at the bar returned to drinking their beer and the workers to eating burgers. The youth scowled at them feeling the impotence in his outrageousness. Stump slipped past and out the door as the boy collected his thoughts in an attempt to get some attention from the adults.

"Leo I believe that boy peed all over himself an the floor, yuh better make Ellen come mop it up before someone falls on their ass."

Leo finally looked up, "Why ain't you in school. Seems like a bunch punks like you otta try spendin some time learnin sumpthin useful, sted uh botherin that poor bastard."

"We quit school. They weren't teachin anything worth knowin up there. After deer season we're headin down to the Cities an make us some real money. An when we come back here watch out. Shit we probly won't even come back, ain't nothin here worth a pinch uh shit."

"Hell in that case why wait for deer season. Greyhound bus runs everyday. Might as well start down that road to prosperity right uh way." Leo's comment finally drew a laugh from the bar.

"We need some Cokes an the balls for the pool table."

"I don't think so, I'm startin uh Veterans only policy, an I'm perty darn sure you ain't no veteran Deak."

"Hell Leo, ain't half the people in here veterans. Yuh gonna kick them out too."

"No. Just you an them two halfwits."

Deak stood there for a second rubbing his well greased hair, trying to find a way to save face in front of his friends, giving up he turned and led the swaggering group through the door.

Stump wandered down the railroad tracks. He stopped for a while and looked out over the charred swamp. His milkweed and thistle hiding place was gone as were the scrub willows where he used to urinate. Only the giant willow that grew over the creek and the evergreens remained. With some of the lower limbs singed back Stump could see the place under the pines where the children had had their fire. He had smelled the smoke when he was returning from helping Sam pull net. He had stopped and watched them play from his hiding spot. Telling anyone that they had started the fire didn't seem right and then he might get in trouble for watching them play. He enjoyed being around children when they didn't tease, but people always got nervous when he was. It really didn't matter. He knew everything would quiet down and something else would soon capture the town's attention. He could ride this out as he had countless other mishaps.

Chapter 16

"Ma! Ma yuh mind if I do some washin?" Peggy looked into her mother's bedroom. It was nearly dark, slits of light streamed in through loosely drawn Venetian blinds. Dust particles suspended in these narrow   bars of brightness started to obey the laws of gravity again and sift through the stale air.

"Ma you wake?"

A lump on the bed stirred, turned from the window and towards the door. A head effected partial separation from the pillow, two reddened eyes squinted out at her from beneath a mat of hair through a room that always smelled of medicine.

"I knew yuh'd come home."

"I ain't stayin. Just din't wanna spend money for washin."

"Well its nice yuh come to visit anyway. I was just uh layin here thinkin bout yer father. Not Mr. Slayton, I mean yer real papa. Oh he was a fine man Peggy uh real gentleman. I just know if I'd uh told him bout you things would uh been different. He'd uh understood an loved yuh. Things would uh been good then. Things would uh been right. None uh this could uh happened with him there to pertect us."

Peggy shifted impatiently. This was the standard in conversation with her mother. A rote lesson that developed siblings, homes, and wealth as the day progressed and the contents of the quart bottle of brandy on the chest of drawers diminished. She would try to convince Peggy that lousy timing had cheated her of this fantasy world and desertion had no part in their circumstances. The other option was the shame of Peggy's father dying in the war, and her not being able to collect a dime in benefits. She didn't seem to remember the letters pleading for help that went unanswered, while the man completed his artillery training, or was it flight school, she had told both versions so often that she wasn't sure which was the truth. Truthful things were covered with a sheet and stuffed back in the corners of her mind, like Stump hiding things he didn't want Ray asking him about in the remotest regions of his closet, they were best covered in dust, forgotten, or discolored   by time.

"Ma I talked to the welfare lady. She got things all fixed for me, even got me a ticket on the afternoon   bus to Minneapolis."

"What yuh goin down there for."

"It's the baby ma." Peggy hesitated for a second. "I'm goin to a home for other girls like me till it's born then I'm gonna give it away."

Mrs. Slayton sat up in bed and glared at her daughter. "Why yuh gonna do that? You made uh mistake now yuh gotta live with it, just like I did." Her angry eyes filled with the alarm and fear which even transient reality caused, her voice had shifted from a rummy haze to sharp and accusing. "Its cuz its Mr. Slayton's ain't it, yer runnin off cuz uh that."

"It ain't his if it was I'd uh gone with Lorna an got it scraped." The immensity of what her mother had just said finally penetrated making her nauseous and dizzy.

"You knew all along he was doin that an yuh din't stop him. I used to think if

I could only somehow let yuh know he'd haf'ta stop. Christ I used to pray yuh'd catch him an we'd get out uh here, an start over where he'd never be able to find us. An here yuh knew an let him. Yuh always made me feel like I ruined yer life. Look whatcha done to mine."

Mrs. Slayton was sobbing now. Sitting half way up in bed supported by a sheet wrinkled arm, crying for something that was real and current. She wanted Peggy to leave so she could banish this to the back of the closet where she thought it was stored with the other unpleasant things, safely wrapped, incapable of hurt, not standing there with an accusing finger pointed her way.

"I never once said you ruined my life. I never said that. Yer father an Mr. Slayton ruined it, ruined it for both of us."

"It don't matter much now. I'm leavin all this shit. The lady say's my baby's gonna have a nice family to take care of it. It's gonna get a chance. The lady say's they'll train me too, get me uh job with a future not just servin food an washin dishes. I ain't ever comin back here."

Peggy turned and walked down the hall. She picked up the suitcase from the floor by the steps leading down into the basement, paused, and then reached out and pushed against the door to her old bedroom slamming it with a bang that echoed through the empty house. She walked down stairs and stuffed her dirty clothes into the washing machine.

Mrs. Slayton looked at the empty doorway where her daughter had been standing. She lay back, turned on her side and watched the dust particles slowly dance in the streaks of light. Peggy was wrong she hadn't known from the start. When Peggy was twelve Mr. Slayton had started being more generous with liquor purchases and less demanding of the sex that had always followed. She had considered herself lucky and generally would pass out several hours after his return from forays through the countryside. She probably would never have known if her bladder would have held the equivalent of her thirst. One night when Peggy was nearly fourteen she had been stricken with the urge. Mr. Slayton was gone and she assumed he had gone into town to drink with the friends he always talked about, but she never met. When she passed Peggy's bedroom on her way to the bathroom she could hear Peggy's softly sobbing, and the wheezing nose snorts that always accompanied Mr. Slayton's orgasm. It was a defining moment in her life. She could have rushed into the room and put an end to the horror for her daughter and re-entered a world of reality. Instead she completed the task she had set out on, returned to her room, and drank the rest of the bottle of brandy. After that she always went to the bathroom before retiring for the night and drank enough to find the haven of sleep.

"I should uh told her father bout her before he shipped out. Things would uh been different then, things would uh been real nice."

It was a whisper that she alone could hear. Truth couldn't enter into here and stay long. It twisted and became something new, harmless, a vapor dancing with the dust in the veiled sunlight.

An hour later Peggy had finished her laundry and was hanging it up on a thin cable stretched between the trees in her mother's backyard. She had fought the memories back, but now outside with the fresh autumn air around her, she looked back into the pain filled walls. At first he had been nice. He had changed from what he had been all through her childhood. Before he had reminded her of her stupidity at every opportunity and made her feel as if she was constantly in his way. Suddenly he was nice, telling her how pretty she was, bringing her gifts from his business trips and telling her that they were just their secret. He would even take her side in the occasional arguments she would have with her mother. Then one night after her mother had staggered to the bedroom he had told her she was getting so grown up he thought it would be all right for her to have a drink. He mixed it up with pop and it had tasted good. After several of these drinks he raped her. He had tried to snuggle and talk sweet. When she resisted he held her down. She had screamed, and fought to no avail, her mother was beyond hearing, and the neighbors were used to hearing loud noises, and fighting from the Slayton house. When she threatened to tell, he told her that nobody would believe her and that she would end up in reform school. She believed him and endured. When she was fifteen she could endure no more, and told him she was going to tell if it didn't stop and that she would rather go to reform school. He quit touching her, but his eyes were always there, moving out had been easy.

The wind whipped the clothes around as she hung them out and the fall sun began drying them. Mrs. Wright stepped out on her back porch and stared at her. She waved and said hello. The older woman didn't respond, but continued to stare. Peggy made an obscene gesture with her middle finger, the way Lorna had shown her, and Mrs. Wright hurried back into her house.

She saw Stump sitting on the bundles of oak shims down by the loading platform. She could see he was staring at her and could almost feel his eyes going over her. It stirred something in her. She had a desire to spurn and reject a town that had never accepted, or helped her, by doing something much worse than the things she had been accused of. He was even more a reject than she, like the Goatman had said they were the same. She decided to go down and talk to him, stir things up, and then leave forever. It wasn't a reasoned response to her life, but very little she did was. She continued to transfer the contents of the basket onto the clothes line using the wooden pins to suspend them in the breeze. Mrs. Wright could be seen through her living room window talking on the telephone and staring at her again. She smiled sweetly and waved. Mrs. Wright turned her back on the girl and continued waving her free hand in an animated discussion with her unseen cohort. One last thing was just what Peggy felt this town needed to sputter about.

Chapter 17

Stump was perched on the rough bundle of wooden shims when the girl came out. He didn't want to watch her, and feared the things he thought when he did. He tried to look away but his eyes always returned to her. She was wearing a brown dress. The one she wore when she waited tables at the restaurant. Her firm roundness pushed at the material as she hung her laundry. She stretched and moved with a grace that warmed him and made his uneasiness unbearable.

A yellow utility vehicle pulled up in front of Stump. The men riding in it jumped out and threw several bails of shims onto the flat bedded cart they were towing. They climbed back into their machine and put-putted down the tracks to the stack of ties. The men grunted and swore as they slid the long creosote soaked logs onto the cart when it was full they started their engine and motored away out of town.

"Whatcha doin Stump"

Stump pulled back as if he had been slapped. She was standing there so close he could touch her. Her brown hair blowing about billowed and tickled his cheek. So close he could smell the flowery perfume that used to waft behind her when she would pass him on the street.

"I seen yuh watchin me. Yuh done it before too. Don't get scared I don't mind, girls like bein watched sometimes."

She moved closer. He could feel the warmth of her body now. She was nearly pressing herself against him. She stood there talking. Saying things about the people in town, and how they were all against her, and how she felt Stump could understand her since they were so mean to him too. His heart was beating so hard he could hear it and feel his pulse in the lobes of his ears. His body trembled with natural feelings he had been conditioned to suppress. He could feel his face grow hot as it turned red, his body felt chilled and detached. She was actually pressing against him now pushing her pelvis onto his knee as she turned casually to one side or the other in her conversation. Her hair moving in the wind kept brushing against his face he inhaled the sweet muskiness of her shampoo. A power beyond his control was moving him. He felt like running, getting away but dormant chemicals were ruling his body, and his mind had surrendered to these other forces. His mother's tutoring words were drowned out by the sweet, soft words the girl said to him. His mother had accepted that his mind would never be up to the responsibilities of the world, but didn't think it proper to explain how his maturing body could find relief for the urges that were a part of maturing. Repression of these desires seemed the only safe course for her son, she had concentrated on that lesson more than any.

"Yuh got such big arms, that's why there so afraid of yuh."

She reached out and caressed his shoulder and down his arm. He was standing now. He was captured by her tiny hand. He gently pulled her back under the planks of the platform, behind the wall of stacked bundles of wooden shims. She giggled nervously in the near darkness. This hadn't been in her plan of upsetting the neighborhood. They couldn't even see her in here. She looked up at Stump knowing that she could reduce him to tears by yelling at him. But he was already crying large wet drops coursed down his cheeks. They glistened as they rolled over the portions of his face that the streaks of sunlight from overhead had illuminated.

Stump stood up first. Wild unreasoning fear in his eyes, he looked like the Anderman's dog had when the train hit it a glancing yet mortal blow. Hind legs not working it had howled and snapped at its rear end as if something foreign was attacking it there.

The deed was done it was too late to change. He was terrified. He stood there above her confused, head moving back and forth between what he had done and what would be its result.

She wiggled around on the ground pulling her underwear back on. She saw the fear but couldn't understand it. Worse things then this had happened to her, there wasn't a crowd of jeering, drunken boys, urging their friends on, no morning after of a leering Mr. Slayton winking at her behind her hung over mother's back. She stood and pulled the front of her dress back down over her legs. She buttoned the front concealing her breasts.

Stump grabbed his coat from the ground and ran out into the painful sunlight. He could feel his father's hard stare and remember his mother's warnings. "Just stay away from the girls Carl. They'll let yuh by with lots, but if yuh touch a girl, they'll put yuh away fast. They'll put yuh away forever if yuh mess with girls". Stump had disobeyed her only once before, with the barmaid. He had been drunk then, out of control. He had no excuse now. Ray wouldn't be able to fix this with the Judge and the Doctors. This must be the rape thing he overheard people say he would end up doing "if sumpthin wasn't done about him", they would send him away or worse for this. He started walking, stumbling over the uneven ties. He started to run.

"It's alright Stump. I ain't gonna tell nobody. Its okay, don't be so scared." She realized suddenly that she was yelling, but that Stump either couldn't hear her, or wasn't listening any more. She looked around. No one was in sight. She looked down the tracks. He was standing above the swamp looking down at the creek. He seemed to be sobbing uncontrollably now. "I shouldn't uh done that if somebody'd seen us I'd never hear the end of it."

She looked up the hill at her mother's house. The clothes on the line appeared to be dry, whipping briskly in the cold Northwest wind which had risen while they had been behind the wall of shims. She hoped that she wouldn't miss her bus. Walking up the hill, picking her way through the patches of dried sand burs, she hugged her arms above her belly and hoped that whoever got her baby wouldn't let it make the mistakes she had. What outrage the Mrs. Wright's of her old neighborhood might feel wasn't worth the pain she knew he was feeling now. She didn't understand why he was so upset. She looked back at the Railroad tracks, "I guess it's cuz he's gotta live here."

The door to the Greyhound Bus hissed hydraulically behind her. She walked up the steps and handed her ticket to the driver. He gave her back a stub for the suitcase full of her earthly possessions he had tossed so unceremoniously into the cargo hold.

She took a seat directly behind the driver, placed her purse on the seat next to her, and looked out the window. Gray clouds had formed a wall to the North and West. The lake was standing on end, an even mixture of white caps, and incredibly cold looking blue, surged back and forth against the stone breakwater. The bus jerked, rudely pulling her into the present, as it moved away from the old depot. As it crossed the tracks she saw Stump carrying a bundle of something, headed out of town, walking more surely than he had before. It was so far she couldn't tell what it was, she couldn't see very clearly. Her house was there, so tiny she could just barely make out her mother's blinded window. Small, and slowly receding, lost now in the tears or maybe it was just the cloud of ash swirling between them out of the swamp.

Chapter 18

A few flakes of snow were falling slanting out of the Northwest wind and melting slowly as they struck the ground. Stump trotted down the tracks towards home, not really aware any more of his steps, wrapped in the fear, consumed by the need to hurry. He passed the old logging road where Alfred had lived for so many winters but didn't see the smoke coming out of his tar paper shanty. He inhaled it in huge gulps in his rush to get away, but like all the scenery on the way to his parent's homestead, he was unaware of the smell of wood smoke. Stump stopped when he reached the cedar swamp that bordered the tracks just before his home fields. He stood there looking down into the Salvation Creek cedars. They existed in eternal twilight, sheltering out the sun, in a gloom where moss could grow so thick that it blanketed the ground, even growing over, and concealing the slow moving stream in places.

He slid down the bank shielding the bundle in front of his chest. The silence here was good. A feeling of calm caught up to him. The first he had felt since he spotted the girl hanging her laundry. His feet were silent as they rose and fell in the soft moss. The indentations left by his passing feet alone marred the smooth, green, velvety cover. It took him just a short time to work his way through the creek meanders to the little island of oaks that towered above the evergreen darkness. Stump sat for a time on a downed limb looking as the snow began to fall faster. He heard something or someone out towards the railroad bed, They must be after him already. He turned his face into the wind and snow and watched it swirl into his face feeling the cold wet sting of life. He thought of his mother as he unwrapped his parcel. Her gentle words surrounded him now, not the lectures he wished he could have listened better to. A rusty twelve gauge shotgun lay in his lap. The falling snow landed on its barrel and melted. He thought he could hear someone cracking through the crust of ice a short distance from him. He was sorry to leave the things and people he liked, but knew that they would take him away from them anyway. He couldn't stand the thought of walls painted a green that nothing living had ever seen, of the daily shuffle for food or toilet and finally bed. This was the only way he could be sure they wouldn't put him away, to grow old safely, where he couldn't live.

The snow continued that night, wet clingy snow, inches of it, covering the bright fallen leaves and late season flowers, blanking out color, making everything the same boring monotone. The only noise was the far off sound of tires on wet pavement, the closer rattle of a dry milkweed pod shaking in the wind, and the murmur of the stream as it gurgled into eternity over the mossy logs.

Chapter 19

He'd almost told them last night. The guilt he felt had kept him awake again, and when he did find sleep, it was so full of horrid dreams that he didn't feel rested. Monsters waited under the steps, and jumped out, or grabbed his ankles from between the treads, as he went down in the dark, into the basement. He would wake up trembling, and then lay still thinking of the fire. Before his wish had been that they hadn't played with fire, but when Stump disappeared he had the added wish that they could have told the truth about who had started it. With less than two days until church he felt a need to confess to someone. But standing in front of his father he lost the courage, and instead of saying what he needed to so desperately, he had asked if he could go deer hunting tomorrow. His father had given him a questioning look, and stated the obvious, and seemingly unnecessary. No one in his family went out hunting deer until they were at least thirteen. Philip knew this and needed no reminders. Standing there he felt more ashamed of not admitting his guilt, when everyone had assumed it was Stump, than he felt for starting the fire. He had to say something, and the sight of his fathers hunting clothes provided him a way out of the room, and away from the look his father was giving him, the look it seemed everyone had for him since his world had grown so complicated. Anne and Tim were keeping away from him and when they did associate together it seemed someone always brought up Stump's mysterious disappearance. For a man who had been invisible to most of the town except for the times he blundered doing something, and someone saw it, his absence caused quite a stir. It was speculated that he had hopped a freight train and would come back when it was warm again. Others were convinced that he had gotten lost in the blizzard on Monday and some hunter would find his body in deer season if they were lucky, and if not, they would just have to watch the crows in the spring. The people that subscribed to this theory repeated it grimly, and with a hard look on there faces, as if they knew something those around them didn't, as if it was something they had warned the community about forever, and it brought them little joy now it had come to pass.

The children dreaded hearing this, but couldn't resist listening whenever they heard a new twist, or of a mysterious sighting.

His welfare worker Ray had looked in all the old spots, and had even reported him missing to the Sheriff. Emma Schwartz told anyone who would listen that he had headed west out of town at three ten Monday afternoon looking mighty suspicious, and carrying something. Leo and Auntie Ellen looked up after the Noon Whistle sounded every day, hoping to get to be the first to tell the other to fry a burger, or pour a beer, because he was here, only to be disappointed by someone else coming through the door.

Philip knew he had run away because of the fire, and prayed that he would turn up alive, and well, but living somewhere else.

This morning, long after his father and brothers had donned the necessary red and left for the woods, Philip had pulled an old red hunting coat on over his clothes and went for a walk down the tracks. On any other opener of deer season he and his two friends would have taken up stations at the junction of Highway 34 and 371, and watched the parade of dead deer coming through town. Like floats on the Fourth of July, they applauded the bucks, and jeered fawns that went by. Tied down to cars, tongues hanging out limply, or stiff in death, depending on how rigidly the hunter adhered to the stricter sense of when season started. Anne and Tim were in Bemidji, and it was hard to have fun with them anymore. Their usual obsession with how to atone for sin had taken a more serious turn once they had done something they actually felt guilt over. It was one thing to come up with ways of getting a blanket forgiveness, which covered stealing candy from Old Man Eikilson, by admitting to the everyday sin of disobeying your parents. The three of them instinctively knew that the only peace they would find from this deed was the truth, but life so far had taught them that small lies were easier to live with than even a just punishment. Both society and their church had made it obvious that courage was less often rewarded then was a well kept secret. The struggle between what they should do, and what they would do, made being together less fun.

It was a bright cold day. The snow that had fallen on Monday was still thick on the ground. Philip bundled against the cold walked along on the butt end of the railroad ties where the snow was gone, rather then slog through the deeper cover to the side of the tracks. As deep in thought as a young boy can be he had walked further from town then he had ever been. He stopped beside a little pond mostly covered in ice. It had frozen after the snow, with its cap reflecting clear blue sky and shores all white, Philip was shaken from his morose ponderings. He stood there looking down at the beauty of the day, and suddenly he knew he had to confess, and that he could confess. Not to the priest in some tricky way that would keep him from shouldering punishment, but to his parents, he would assume all the blame and leave his friends out of it, maybe then he could feel good again.

His decision made he did feel better. The burden seemed gone and the shiny ice invited him to try some sliding. He plowed down the bank to the pond. Testing the ice near shore with a firm stomp, first with one foot, and then with both, satisfying his limited concerns for safety. He was soon running and sliding on the smooth surface. Through the transparent cover he could see the rocks and logs sticking up from the weedy bottom. He trusted the ice, but caution kept him close to what he perceived to be the safety of shore. Taking rocks from the northern shore where the sun had kept them warm enough to melt the snow, he chopped through the surface, and saw that where he was playing there was at least two inches of ice. Giving the rocks a toss he watched them slide out towards the bit of open water near the middle of the pond. They gave a satisfying plop as they went over the edge. A Ring Bill duck swam to the far side of the opening. Alone and wounded with a piece of lead from a shotgun, it waited the encircling tomb of ice.

Philip grew tired of slipping and falling down, and decided to walk over to the beaver house to see what their mound of logs looked like from close up. As he drew nearer the den his view of the bottom became a thicket of limbs and twigs, all enmeshed in one another, the clear water beneath him seemed to be deeper. Shore was still close at hand and the beaver house nearly touchable now so he still was sure of his safety. Even when the ice gave out the first brittle sounds of cracking beneath his feet, he was still sure everything was okay. It started to sag and he was frozen in a fear that came on more suddenly than his earlier feeling of redemption.

When it gave way to his weight things went so fast that his last breath was a hopeless gasp of some air, but mostly water. Down he went into the freezing water, his upturned screaming face let go the bubbles of air he had captured prior to immersion. They trickled up to the surface, and worked their way to the edges of the hole his body had made in the ice on its way down. He would have come up but he was caught tight in the sticks of the beavers feed bed. The current created by the busy rodents had kept the ice here by their food supply thin, and the branches firmly tucked into the muddy bottom completed the trap, which held captive Philip's foot, and consequently the rest of his thrashing body.

He looked up at the glowing surface, and saw the sun narrow down until it was surrounded by the hole he had made. The darkness drew in around him, and he wasn't sure if he was trying to escape from sleep and the dream phantoms that grabbed him from beneath basement stairs, or if this nightmare was real. His hole was gone now, only a point of intense light remained. The hand of God penetrated the light. The last thing he saw was it reaching down, with its dirty, chewed off, fingernails.

Chapter 20

When Philip woke up the worst of his fears had been realized. He was in a hot, foul smelling, dark place, with smoke burning his eyes, and the dead Stump standing above him with a terrible expression on his face. When he saw the light of recognition return to the boy's face Stump smiled and extended a large hand tipped with gnawed off nails, and brushed back a wisp of hair, which partially obstructed one eye. The boy looked behind Stump, to the single dirty window which provided the only light to the shack. The trees beyond the glass were filtering a low reddish glow, but he had no idea if the sun was setting or rising, if it was still Saturday, or if a week had passed.

"Yuh broke the ice where dem beavers swim to get sticks an stuff to eat. I got wet tryin to reach down to where yuh was stuck. Yuh hungry? I'm awful hungry there ain't much food here, an he hides what there is, I'd give pertinear hundred dollars for uh hambugger an some tator soup, an maybe some chili an uh fry pie, yer Momma still make rhubarb cake. Man that was good cake! My Ma all the time said that Missus Anderman makes the best rhubarb cake in the whole world, we use to eat lots then. It's uh good thing dem buttons held, I was scared they'd come off an I'd yank yer jacket clean off yuh an there'd yuh'd be drownded. I could eat five whole chickens an tators an gravy, I din't eat since this mornin an only some old bread then. Yer back sore? I had to whop yuh cuz yuh was blue an wouldn't breath, hope I din't hurt yuh, bout six times, then that brown pond water comes pourin outta yer mouth, an yuh started gaggin an coughin. I runned back here quick. We was both pertinear solid ice, an it was perty damn cold here too cuz he's so stingy with his wood, even though I saws it, cuts it, an hauls it, he yells evertime I try to throw uh hunk in the stove. I din't think yuh'd ever wake up."

A door opened letting in more light and a beastly cold wind. The Goat Man and Sam Cloud entered what now appeared to the boy to be an incredibly dirty room. They both dumped arm loads of wood on the floor beside a glowing barrel stove.

"He woke up an started lookin round, first he just laid there breathin funny an moanin, then his eyes opened up an he looked scared. So I talked to him, an he don't look so scared no more."

"Yuh ain't had a bath in a week no wonder he's scared." Sam said this and walked up to the mattress Philip found himself laying on. "Didn't yer father teach yuh better'n to go walkin around uh beaver house?"

Philip was too stunned by the strange surroundings to respond.

"It's a damn good thing he got tired of this one's bull shit an went for a walk or you would uh been keepin company with the beavers all winter." Sam reached down and felt the boys face. "He warmed up good enough I guess. Yuh got anything to drink in here."

Alfred glared at Stump, reached behind the stove and extended a bottle of cheap brandy. Stump glared back at Alfred.

"You said yuh'd spent it all on food if I give yuh my money. I been starvin to death an you got booze."

"Yer my guest here yuh know, an its just fair that yuh pay yer fair share since I opened my home to yuh." He continued to extend the bottle towards Sam.

"Not booze for Christ sake, yuh wanna kill him? Any water or sumpthin that doesn't have stuff growin in it."

Stump went over to the table and picked up a crusty cup, looked into it and dumped the contents onto the dirt floor. He then walked to the stove and used his coat sleeve to grab the handle of what had once been a blue enamel coffee pot. Philip sat up, took the offered cup, and sipped in a mouth full of the bitter, hot liquid. He learned after the first sip to use his teeth to strain out the grounds, and other bits of matter, which were suspended in the coffee. Sitting up he realized that the mattress was where the bad smell came from. The air in the room smelled of wood smoke. The walls had catalog pictures of women in their underwear stuck to them with thumb tacks. Piles of old clothes and stacks of magazines covered most of the floor.

"I'm sorry," Philip paused, "I, us, it was me. That started the fire, I done it. I was playing with a fire down by the swamp, an it was me. Then they all blamed you, but I knew it was me, an then I din't do nothin. I'm sorry yuh had to leave town when it was me that done it."

Stump shrugged his shoulders and smiled, "I saw yuh down in them trees. It don't matter bout no fire, I know'd who started it. I figgered for sure you was dead when yuh plunked through the ice, but I took yuh here to Alfred hopin he could help yuh, an then Sam was here cuz he figgered out where I was hidin, so here we all are." He smiled again and sat down on a poplar log next to the mattress on the floor.

Sam looked at Alfred who looked back and seemed to be just as confused by the conversation as he was. Sam had stopped by the shack thinking the disappearance of Stump might in some way be connected with Alfred's move back to the woods. Stump was gone, but Alfred had readily admitted that Stump had been there, and had only left minutes before, due to a misunderstanding about the property rights to a small container of potted beef. The meat in question had been purchased with Stump's funds, but Alfred reasoned that as long Stump was afraid to go into town that he should decide when to eat it, since he would have to go in the next time for food and beverage. He had told Sam of seeing Stump go by when he had been out sawing wood just before the snow on Monday. Stump was carrying something, and Alfred told Sam he suddenly got worried for his friend. Sam suspected that Alfred was as curious about the potential of the bundle as he was worried about Stump, but didn't bring it up. Alfred told of finally finding Stump curled up and hiding under a huge oak tree with an empty shotgun beside him. Stump had told him the entire story of the girl and his fears of being locked up again, and about the shotgun. He had led him back to the shack and had kept him there not knowing if the girl had made up a story about Stump, or if it would be safe for his friend to go home. He had gone into town with some of Stump's money but heard so many rumors about his disappearance that he decided to keep him for a while. Sam felt sure at least until Stump's small stash of money was gone.

Stump owed his life once again to his mother. A decision she had made when he was just a boy had crossed time and saved him. She had asked his father to not teach him about guns from fear of an accidental shooting. Stump knew how to pull back the hammer and use the trigger but it had never dawned on him that he needed to see if there was a shell in the chamber.

Alfred took a long sip from his bottle and then slid it back into its place of concealment behind the wood stove. Sam didn't drink, and Stump wasn't big on hard liquor, but he thought it would be just like Stump to re-hide the booze to punish him for spending food money on something someone else might want. He reached over to the strand of wire he had stretched near the stove to hang the boys wet clothes on. They were dry to the point of being hot to touch. "Yuh did better'n most would kid, I think I'd uh shit my drawers, hung up in uh feed bed like that. Just remember who saved yer skinny ass." He nodded towards Stump and started tossing the boy's clothes to the mattress. Using a small stick of wood he lifted the latch on the stove door and pulled it open with a rusty metallic squeak. He tossed in several chunks of Jack Pine, the bark and sap started to pop and crackle before he could close the stubborn door.

Philip embarrassed pulled some of his clothes on under the scratchy wool blanket they had wrapped him in. With his bottom half covered he crawled out of the smelly bed and stood by the chugging wood stove, turning first one side, and then other towards the heat as he donned the remainder of his garments. The stove's thin barrel sides were orange in places from heat and short tongues of flame licked from the air vent. It made a wonderful clicking sound which accompanied the "whump whump whump", of the small bursts of escaping fire. Philip looked around the room. Flattened cardboard boxes had been nailed to the assortment of boards and small logs which held the roof up. Pin-up girls with their tops exposed, bottoms casually wrapped in towels, as if they had just stepped out of showers or baths, looked down from the filthy paper walls. The top of the barrel stove had been hammered almost flat and the coffee pot sat there steaming away. On the nearest wall under a page of Sear's bra ladies, a cast iron frying pan and bean encrusted kettle hung from nails. Philip's attention went back to a nearby Miss August. Alfred made a honking snort and spit a large wad of snot and brownish goo onto the upper side of the glowing barrel. It hissed and danced away into steam, just inches from the grimy coffee pot. Philip had a queasy feeling, remembering the horrible tasting liquid he had so recently drank. Where ever his eyes went they seemed either to end up falling on half naked ladies or to travel back to the now dehydrated lung matter. He sat on a large pine log turned end up and marred by the countless hatchet blows it took to create kindling for fires in a cold stove. His socks felt warm and good as he pulled them on, and the green rubber of his insulated boot was almost too hot to the touch.

"Where's my other boot? I can only find the one of em."

Alfred laughed. "Down in the loon shit I spose. Stump pulled yuh right out uh yer boot. I spose we could take yuh back an yuh could try fishin it out but yuh'd get all wet agin."

"My Ma's gonna kill me. Them boots was bran new this fall."

Sam felt the boys red jacket. "I better get this boy home his folks'll be goin nuts missin him by now."

"Yuh think yer pickup can make it down the trail from the road."

"Never do it, even without snow it'd get hung up in that big hole where yuh go round the end of the cedar swamp. Some uh them sumac up on top are as big as small trees now, an my truck don't have much push left in it."

" Well have Stump carry him, get em both outta here, I swear to Christ he's worse'n the goats. All the time pissin an moanin bout no food, too hot, too cold, or me wantin to spend all his money, an snore, my god, bout rips the walls down when he sets to. Then he thinks I should share my mattress an get new blankets, cuz he thinks these stink. Yea it'd be lots better to take him back too."

"I ain't goin back, Sam, they'll make me go away to the state hospittle again, an Ray ain't gonna come get me, cuz uh what I done."

"They ain't gonna bother yuh Stump. Alfred told me what yuh said happened with the girl. I heard she left town, went down to the cities. If she'd uh said yuh hurt her I would uh heard bout it in a week. You carry the boy an lets get while there's still light to see the trail by."

"Yuh sure they'll leave me alone?"

"I promise specially when they hear bout yuh savin the boy. Shit yer a hero, probbly make the six uh clock news, get to shake the mayors hand an everything."

The men wrapped the boy in several burlap bags smelling of musky earth instead of the pervasive odor of decay that clung to Alfred's blankets.

Sam looked across the shack at Alfred who stood quietly by his glowing stove. "You comin with us?"

"Hell no! I don't need no punk kid welfare worker tryin to tell me what's right for me. Sneakin round, askin bout what I do, an how I spend my own damn money. You see him tell him to shove the lithium up." He looked at the boy. "Tell him to take the damn poison himself, if it's so damn good for uh person."

Stump easily picked Philip up and they trudged off down the snow filled trail.

Alfred watched until they had disappeared then sighed and pulled the door shut. He dug the bottle of brandy out of its hiding spot behind the stove, and took a long drink. Sitting down on the only chair in his shack, he watched the bit of fire that could be seen through the air draft. The dark of loneliness closed in around him, just as surely as the water of the beaver pond had surrounded the boy earlier, only there were no hands available to pull him out. He'd sent them away, as he had always sent them away. Looking back on his life it hadn't just been the one big blow that had set him on the path to this place. It had been a million annoying taps. A pain in his chest seized him, he grimaced, coughed, and spit onto the stove. Glancing into the corner where Stump's attempt at escape leaned harmlessly, and forgotten, he thought about saving some money out of his next check to buy a box of shells. Outside the wind moaned through the trees, and mixed the ascending smoke of Alfred's fire, into the air, with huge flakes of snow that had begun to fall.

Chapter 21

Mrs. Anderman pulled back the edge of the rooster print curtain, and looked down the snow packed path that led out of their yard, and to the street. For the hundredth time since this morning, when she had watched Philip's red parka draped figure disappear into the glittering frost filled day, the trail was empty. It was late. The sun was already getting quite low in the sky. She had determined to ground the boy mid-afternoon when he hadn't return for lunch, as he had promised. Thoughts of giving the grilled cheese she was saving for him, to Pat the neighbor's Labrador, and make Philip go to bed hungry had even crossed her mind. She dropped the curtain edge, walked over to the phone, and dialed a number she had memorized about an hour after lunch time had come and gone.

"Hello." Mrs. Peterson's tired voice answered.

"Hi Emma this is Ruth Anderman. Is Philip with you?"

"No we been in Bemidji all day, seein the baby, an she is so cute, you just wouldn't believe how darling that little thing is."

Normally Mrs. Anderman would have listened the appropriate length of time to the bragging of a new Aunt, but she had called all of Philip's friend's mothers. This was the last and best chance she thought she had of tracking him down, short of calling in the police. "I'm sorry Emma, but I gotta ask did Philip come by there at all this mornin, maybe you could ask yer kids if they might know where he's at."

"Ann! You know where Philip Anderman might be?" In the background there was a muffled reply. " No he didn't come by here. Sorry Ruth, but Ann said last she saw him was the other day in school. How longs he been gone?"

"Since this morning. He said he was goin to play, an I told him to be home for lunch, an I called everyone. I just was hopin that he went somewhere with you, cause I kept callin an there wasn't an answer. If he comes by there call me right away." Mrs. Anderman picked up the phone book and turned to the front page where the emergency numbers were listed. In the distance she heard, the backfiring of her husband's pickup as he down shifted coming off the highway. She set the directory down, walked back to the window, pulled back the curtain, and prayed. Just how she wasn't sure, but somehow Philip had to have found her husband and the boys out hunting. He knew the way out to the old homestead, everything would be all right again. The truck would pull up in front of the house, and the boys would be piled in two deep on the bench seat, crammed in, and laughing about the cramped quarters. When it came it was crammed, but not enough, three boys and her husband climbed out and stood by the back of the pickup looking at something in the box. She ran out of the house sobbing the tears she had fought with all day. Alone no longer, the horrible scenes she had been able to put off as ridiculous, now seemed all too possible, and her happy conclusions had all disappeared.

Mr. Anderman looked up from the dead deer laying insides propped open in the back of his pickup. Something was terribly wrong. His wife never ran and seldom cried. To see both at the same time was the portent of disaster. His first thought was that something had to have happened to John. There had been trickles on the news about advisors over there being killed, but on a ship he had assumed that his oldest was safe. The boys were still too excited by Fred's first deer to look up from it's now stiffening body, and see their mother's pain, or there father turn pale. He went to meet her, before he was half way to her she started speaking .

"Did yuh see Philip anywhere, he was sposed to come back for lunch, but he didn't, I called everyone an told em to call me if they saw him, maybe he's down by the creek, he's always playin down there. Send the boys down there John, have em look real good, an by the loading platform, sometimes them bums hang around waitin for a freight to catch, or maybe sumpthin fell on him, and he's been layin there trapped all day. I told him to be here for lunch, and I just been worried sick. Waiting for someone to call, and say they saw him, or for him to come walkin down the path."

Mr. Anderman held his wife as all of her fears found voice.

"He was wearin red when he left here, and he knows better'n to go out in the woods, but he wanted to go with yuh so bad that he might uh been tryin to find yuh , maybe he got shot, them stray bullets travel so far, maybe he's wounded out in the woods. Or if he went down to watch the cars for deer some one might uh made him get in with em. He's been gone way to long. Send the boys out looking John. We should call the sheriff don't yuh think."

"What's wrong Ma?" Fred asked. He had managed to stop looking at the deer, and wanted to tell his mother the gruesome details of its final moments of life. He had repeated the story to each of his brothers as they came out of the woods, and the shot he had made became more difficult each telling. By sixth hour study hall on Tuesday he would need something more than a single shot twelve gauge and a slug to make his story possible. He had never seen his mother cry and his thoughts of glory disappeared. Soon Tom and Frank stood behind him, all five now single file on the narrow walkway.

"Philip took off this morning and hasn't come back." Mr. Anderman said. His wife now stood sobbing in her husbands arms.

The contentment and happiness they had been feeling because of a successful start to their hunting season died in that fertile region between a person's shoulders and waist, where strong emotions establish instant roots. Arms that had had strength to do anything now felt heavy with the weight of guns and lunch packs. Their mouths had ached from all the laughter and smiling during their crowded ride home. Now their faces were fixed in shock and pain. Philip, who had never been out of contact with at least one of them for more than several hours during school days, was missing in below-zero weather with night well on the way. Each stood desperately searching for a solution, a simple, quick explanation to set them free of the fear their mother had been fighting all day.

Mr. Anderman looked up into the sky and felt the light flakes touch his cheeks. Each breath stung the lining of his nose. "Lets go in an get rid of this stuff, an figger out where to start lookin. I'll call the sheriffs an see if they can send someone to help."

83

Fred's trophy forgotten they walked on the squeaky snow to the house.

The phone was ringing before Mr. Anderman could open the door, his wife rushed to it and briefly the family felt that there might be a reprieve from their gloom.

"Hello! No, No, and yer kids didn't either, well if yuh hear anything call, someone will be here in case he shows up." Mrs. Anderman hung up. "That was just Mrs. Phelps wantin to know if he showed up yet. I must uh called twenty people so I spose the phone'll be ringin all night."

Her crying had stopped. With reinforcements someone else would have to sit and wait his possible homecoming. She could take the car and at least drive around looking for her boy. The horribly disheartening routine of staring out the window, watching the slow sweep of the clock's hands reach a point in time that she was sure would mark his return, eyes going back to the window, stepping outside to blow the tin horn into an unresponsive world, and then finally thinking of the one home she hadn't called but was positive he would be at, was over.

Mr. Anderman walked to the phone, flipped back the cover of the directory, and dialed the county sheriff's office. "Hi Mel. This is John Anderman. Yea we did, my boy Fred got his first. Uh nice big fawn. Just thirteen. Yea it's a perty big deal." He could see the impatience building with the polite chatter in his wife's face. "The reason I'm callin Mel is my youngest has been missin since this morning. He was supposed to be back by noon. Philip, ten years old. Red parka. Yea that's how we spell it. Someone will be by the phone, the rest of us'll be out lookin."

"They haven't heard anything about any strangers hangin round town have they?" Mrs. Anderman asked, sensing that her husband was rushing through even this phone call.

"You hear that Mel? Yea she's perty shook. Sure. I know. We'll call if anything happens here. Yea. Bye."

"He said its deer season, an the woods are full uh people from the cities, but he ain't heard bout anyone kookier then usual showin up." Mr. Anderman turned to his two older boys, "Tom, you an Frank go down by the tracks an look around them box cars they got pulled over on the side rails, and under the loading ramp. If yuh don't find nothin there, look by the creek, an up town. If he ain't there come home an we'll figger out where to look next. Fred, you ride with yer mother, an do any lookin around on foot she might need. Ruth why don't you stop by here every half hour or so in case we hear sumpthin? I'll stay here to watch the telephone. Fred yuh better give me that heart an liver. If yuh forget it it'll be perty ripe in uh day or so. I'll get it all ready an we'll fry it up after yuh bring that little nincompoop home."

Fred tried awkwardly to reach into the game pouch in the back of the oversized hunting coat, but his arms seemed too short. Tom grabbed him, and slid his hand into the slit like opening. He withdrew a Red Owl bread bag dripping a small amount of blood, and containing a soft, heavy substance. The bottom edge of his coats hem was a wetter shade of red.

"John will be real happy with yuh for just single baggin deer guts in his brand new jacket." Tom said as he cupped the gruesome bag with his hand and walked to the sink. He dumped it out and started picking hairs, bits of leaf, and twigs from the stilled organs. They were warm, a strange combination of the fading heat from the now dead fawn, and the warmth of his little brothers back. He turned on the cold water and scrubbed the heart, and then the liver, rinsing the plant matter and dirt in a reddish swirl from the white sink. He grabbed Fred, who had come to the sink to observe, and roughly dried his hands on the back of the borrowed coat. Looking across the kitchen he could see out the window, and into the portion of night the nearest street lamp illuminated. Large snow flakes swept through the beam of light. His eyes shifted to his father and they shared a look of concern which seemed to contradict his apparent nonchalance.

"We better take the good flashlight. It's awful dark down by them box cars an even darker under the loading platform."

Frank nodded his agreement and walked to the basement door, opened it, and reached over to the top of the first support beam, where the most functional flashlight was kept ready for the constant war with the antiquated fuse box.

The two older boys pulled their hats tight down around their ears, and quietly left the house, going out into what was fast becoming a storm.

Chapter 22

It was dark and the snow seemed heavier, falling from the sky, and blowing from the near by cedar bows, in a wind that made the few degrees below zero feel like forty below. Philip's bootless foot felt numb.

"You doin ok kid?" Sam asked from a few feet ahead in the night.

"I can't hardly feel my foot no more."

A hand came out of the dark and felt his cotton socked toes. "Stump un-button one of the buttons on yer coat and stick his foot up in yer armpit. We can't be much more'n uh mile from the road now. We'll be warm in no time if my damn truck starts."

Stump tucked the boy's foot up snug into his underarm and could feel the icy toes wiggle in appreciation of the warmth. The two men trudged through the wintry night, down the seemingly invisible forest trail. Philip shrouded in the potato bags, carried high in Stumps arms looked backwards, keeping his face out of the sharpness of the wind that his guide and bearer had no choice but to face. The dark cedars were blacker than the night looming beyond the narrow edge of the path, huge threatening shapes that appeared, and disappeared, with each of Stumps long strides.

Particles of wind driven snow stung Stump's cheeks, and then mixed with the collection of snot and frozen breath forming a mat like icicle, that clung to the long whiskers surrounding his mouth. It grew thicker with each burst of steam, until his nose and lips were one in a mass of grisly ice. He could feel the trail start to rise in front of him, and instead of cedars to his right the trees were a mixture of naked hardwoods. Stump suddenly felt the full force from a wind the cedars had been at least partially protecting him from. If Sam hadn't been in the lead he would have snuck back into the swamp and curled up out of the wind in the shelter of the trunk and protruding roots of an ancient tree. Waiting out the storm he would have frozen to death, but he could think only of the more level ground and slight shelter of the evergreens.

Sam was waiting in the dark with his eyes clenched to mere slits. Stump nearly stumbled into him. "It's about two hundred yards to the top uh this hill, an there's uh curve to this side." He tapped Stump's left shoulder. "The brush is perty thick there so if yuh get confused an can't see the trail no more, look into the wind, I'm gonna run ahead an get the truck started, an I'll turn the head lights on, so yuh should be able to see them from that bend. Don't go wandering off in the woods. If yuh feel twigs slapping yer face, that means yer off the trail, so stop there an wait for me, or look for my lights. By the time you get there the truck'll be startin to warm up." Sam's silhouette turned and rapidly disappeared into the area of lesser darkness which seemed to be the path.

Stump stood there for a second catching his breath. As skinny as Philip was, his arm felt tired. "I gotta move yuh to my udder side." He tried to keep the bags wrapped around the boy in the arm to arm transfer, but they slipped down from around his head, and the hood pulled back to reveal a few inches of the top of Philip's head to the air and snow. With the boy on his right side Stump was at least somewhat protected from the wind. He returned to the slow trip up hill. In gentler seasons rain and even the snow which punished them now, when turned to water, would trickle down this slope, and collect with the rusty moisture seeping from the dozens of tiny springs on the margin of the hardwoods and the cedar swamp. Once in the cedars it would slowly join together and become the Salvation Creek, flow out of the low evergreens, into the beaver pond which had nearly ended Philip's life, and eventually make its way to the lake they both lived by. The miracle of this arrangement wouldn't have impressed either of them on this winter night. In this area of glacial debris the hills weren't extremely long but they were steep, and in the dark with a wind from Canada trying to turn them around, it seemed a forever hill. The electrician's tape which he was sure, if wrapped just right, would hold the sole of his boot on, and save the dollar Mr. Botts would have charged him for sewing, gave up its hold. It flopped up and down keeping silent cadence to his steps, until snow packed the gap between wool sock and leather. Leo had given him the tape and told him to get it sewed properly. That had been just over a week ago, when the weather knew it was still autumn. If things would have been different, and the adhesive had parted on one of Stump's normal forays into the community, he would have cheerfully gone to Mr. Botts. He enjoyed sitting in the warm little shop waiting his turn, smelling the oiled leather, and listening to the old man talk to the constant stream of loggers and farmers who brought in things in need of repair. Hearing Mr. Botts complain of shoes built so cheaply people threw them away to have new ones, instead of holding onto the traditional, frugal values of the immigrant pioneers. It was one of his winter spots. When he tired of the bars, or watching his ceiling respond to snow melt, he would take a jacket or a glove to the shoe maker and watch as the self employed men of industry took turns ahead of his, and listen to the electric thumping of a dying trade. He would watch people scurry back and forth in the cold, merchants shake their fists as passing plows filled in jealously guarded paths, and their clerks take up shovels to clear the dirty walls of snow tossed up by the road crews indiscriminate blade. On a good day he had long waits for a small repair.

The lump of snow, compacted by his body weight, and what heat there was left in his foot, had been transformed into a chunk of ice. Stepping down on it was no longer painful, but still his steps with his right foot were noticeably shorter than the ones with his left foot. Combined with the shifting of Philip to his right shoulder it was understandable that he encountered brush slapping his face while still on the hill, and long before the turn in the road Sam had warned him of. His veering to the west had taken him off the trail many yards before the branches alerted him to his predicament. The error was understandable but windy winter nights are unforgiving. Stump ever obedient, hurting from a sudden stinging brush poke to his freezing nose, faced the shifting wind and watched for lights.

Chapter 23

By the time he reached the corner where the sumacs had taken over most of the signs of a path, Sam had misgivings about his decision. Too many things could go wrong in the dark. Both the snow and the wind had increased. It was hard to keep his face pointed forwards, but that was the direction he needed to look to stay on the trail. Stump would have a harder time doing this carrying the boy. His thoughts at the bottom of the hill weighed too heavily towards the need to warm Philip back up, and not enough to all the problems that could develop when you don't stay together in the woods. He paused a second, and then pushed on, towards the truck. While he walked and tried to make his eyes see the difference between trail and thin places in the stand of brush, he thought back to the first time he had spoken with Stump.

Every month he took his mother on the long drive down to Brainerd, to visit his sister Angie. He would stand next to his mother as she sat dabbing little drops of drool from the corner of Angie's mouth, speaking softly to her in Ojibwa. She lived on the Medically Fragile Ward of the state hospital, and had been there for many years. Her mind perpetually frozen at about six months, her body had grown far too big for Sam's mother to care for. Sam was convinced that to Angie one care giver was much the same as the next, his mother was sure she relaxed more when she felt and heard family, but with his father dead the only logical choice was this. After about an hour of watching his mother go through her monthly ordeal, he would go out and smoke by the pickup. It was on one of these walks through the labyrinth of wards that he saw Stump standing by the exit door watching him. He knew him by sight only, this big hulking man whose seemingly aimless wanderings were hard to miss in a small town. Stump didn't say anything at first, he just stood there by the door smiling at a familiar face. Sam decided to stop and talk to him. He ended up asking permission to take Stump out on the veranda for a smoke. Several weeks later when a free Stump spotted him on the streets of home he realized he had made a friend for life. It suited Sam. Men he had been close to in Korea went the way of most war time friends, alive only in memories. Being on the road most of the year working construction seemed to complete a solitariness his disposition had consigned him to. He saw a way through Stump to help where he couldn't help in his own family, and in doing this he discovered a friend. He met Alfred in the parking lot at the hospital several months later. The mentally ill were kept in a separate building and Alfred six months away from alcohol, on his medications, well fed, and rested was nearing discharge. He too recognized Sam, but not at all shy bummed a cigarette, and a light. Alfred was annoying at times, but he also could be very funny, and he had some rather harsh insights into existence that were interesting to listen to, in small doses.

In the distance a car passed by on the county road. With the wind he couldn't hear it but their lights danced back and forth through the trees. Flickering until they crossed in front of him, and then a moment of twin head lights as it crossed in front of what little path there was. He relaxed a little. In a few minutes he should have the truck running, and if Stump wasn't quick to show up he could always leave it running and go back to help him find the way. The wind carried snow at him sideways now. Another car passed and he saw the brief outline of his pickup. Encouraged he started to walk faster and was rewarded with a branch stabbing the corner of his eye. He slowed back down and once again felt through the brush with a mitten'd hand leading his way.

Rita would be calling his mother by now. Finding out that there was a nice fat doe hanging in the wood shed, and that there was no reason to worry about her husband being so late. Mother would tell her about his theory on the whereabouts of the missing Stump, and Rita understanding Sam's sense of duty, would go about getting the boys ready for bed, and reassure them that Dad wouldn't be there to say good night, but unlike in the summer, he would be home when they woke up in the morning. Hunting with his cousins earlier in the day had reminded him of how good it felt to be a part. Even though he hadn't lived near them for years they told stories of his, and their, mistakes and triumphs during the annual autumn ritual of bringing in winter meat. They reached out and brought him in with reminders that he was family. Whenever he drove away from his mothers little house he was torn by the need to belong to his past, and the desire to have more than the absolute poverty living in it would mean for his family.

The cab of the pickup sealed out wind and snow and its motor started after a few stubborn grunts and moans. The heater fan in its permanent winter position of full blast, ground up, and spit out bits of autumn leaf, and pine needle. Sam felt much warmer just sitting in the shelter. He turned on the lights. With the snow blowing by it looked like he was slowly backing up. Stump should have reached the crest of the hill where the bend in the road was, if he stopped and looked, the headlights would guide him to the truck. Knowing that November could give them a few warm days, Sam hadn't slipped the mandatory scrap of cardboard between his grill and radiator, fearing that this quick warm up method in decent weather could overheat his engine. It would take at least ten minutes before the engine air blew warm enough that he could shed his mittens. He sat and watched the passing snow and listened to his truck motor reach a reassuring idle rumble. He turned on the dome light and looked at his watch. Six o-clock and already so dark the trees weren't even shapes any more with the truck lights off. So black out that telling east from west or up from down was just guess work. The flashlight he used for netting lay on the seat next to him. Safe from his boy's unquenchable fascination with it and the million reasons they found for using up batteries. The blower air seemed to be warmer. Sam picked up the flashlight and stepped back out into the cold. Stump might be turned around down there by the curve. With this wind the natural inclination would be to turn your eyes at least a little away from the sting, and he might be looking the wrong direction to see the light. As he walked through the sumac in the bath of light from his truck the old road was easy to see. He could also see the blowing snow slowly filling up the edges of his ten minute old tracks. It wasn't as bad walking with wind at his back, the turned up wool collar of his hunting coat and turned down ear flaps blocked out the icy snow, and it seemed to propel him forward. He kept checking the ground in front of him for tracks of Stump, thinking that he might have missed the turn and could be wandering back and forth seeking the trail. The further he walked from the truck and its light the more difficult it became to tell his footprints from the surrounding snow.

At the turn in the trail where the path started it's descent to the cedar's he stopped to look back. He couldn't hear his truck over the wind, but his lights were plain to see. If Stump had gotten this far he would have noticed them. With his back to the wind he stood at the crest of the hill and clicked his flashlight on. He pointed it down hill into the woods, flicking it up and down or side to side and then holding it steady for a few seconds. Starting with what he remembered as being the left side of the trail he worked to the far left in the direction he had told Stump the trail turned. Occasionally he called out, but with the noisy moaning and whistling in the trees he realized it was pointless. Slower this time he worked his way back to the trail allowing longer pauses, while he prayed for the light to be seen. For the thousandth time he regretted parting with the other two. When his beam got back to where he thought the trail was he gave up on them seeing his puny point of light and walked down the hill, looking back until he could no longer see the truck lights.

In the bitter cold the sumac tops broke off easily. He snapped them just below their dull red seed clusters, but left them hanging on the branches. With his light he could see where he thought the trail was. He went down the hill breaking all the seed pods off, marking the corner in the path where he anticipated trouble on his return. When he was clear of the sumac he turned and shined his flashlight up the hill. The red globs hanging down at an unnatural angle stuck out well, pointing to the trail. If his batteries held out he wouldn't have any trouble finding the tricky corner.

Satisfied he turned and walked slowly down towards the cedars, probing the ground with his light and occasionally seeing remaining bits of his tracks in places which were protected from the wind driven snow. Every few yards he would stop and shine his light to the sides and yell Stump's name. When he reached the bottom of the hill he could see the spot where they had parted company, clear dimples in the snow where he had stood and tapped Stump on the shoulder warning him of the turn ahead. Somehow he had missed sign of Stump leaving the trail. He had been searching the left side of the trail as he had descended to the swamp, and hadn't seen anything other than a track he was sure was his now and then, that had somehow escaped being filled in with snow. His only option was to search the right side now and if that didn't produce something to go for help. It was too cold to wait much longer.

About half way up the hill he saw it. A partly obscured boot imprint going slightly to the right just off to the edge of the trail. He slowed down his search and squatted down on his heals. Closer to the snow he could see another unnatural scuff a few feet further on. He got up and walked to it and sank down again and peered at the ground. He saw another track further ahead and sheltered by a tree trunk. Stump was clearly off the trail, heading to the right.

The woods were open here. Mature oaks and maples, huge trees that could choke out the underbrush by sucking up all the sunlight with their tall spreading canopies. Limbs in this type of forest didn't even start sticking out of the trees until they were high enough off the ground to compete with their neighbors for sun. High enough off the ground that Stump would wander for a long time before he hit brush or branches that would tell him he was off the trail.

Chapter 24

Stump's veering pace had taken him into a wind fallen oak tree. After standing frozen for a few minutes Philip turned his head around to see what had stopped their forward progress.

"Why'd yuh stop?"

"There's twigs hittin me. Sam said if yuh run into twigs, yuh gone wrong an to stop right there, an not go wanderin round. Just stay put an look for the lights."

Philip stared long at the obstruction ahead of them. "It looks like a big tree the wind flipped over. I can see uh bunch uh branches an uh log over to the right."

Stump turned. "I don't see nuthin."

"I can it ain't very far, just uh little ways, an I bet yuh can get outta the wind there."

Stump thought about the proposal for a second, but the temptation of getting out of the wind proved stronger than Sam's advice to not move. "Ok but we gotta look for lights."

The trunk of the tree was horizontal to the hill. Suspended three feet above the snow by several thick limbs which had hit the ground first as it fell. One of the branches came out at enough of an angle that Stump could sit quite comfortably on it, completely sheltered from the wind, by the elevated tree trunk, and the snow drift that had formed on the up hill side of the obstruction. By stomping his feet around a little he felt fairly comfortable in comparison to the exposure to the blizzard he had been facing since the cedar swamp. He continued holding the boy on his lap with Philip's bootless foot tucked under the coat flap up by his belly.

"Do I smell like uh dump?"

"Huh?"

"Like the song dem kids all'uh time sing, Stump, Stump smells like uh dump someone should tell him tuh wipe his rump, rump. I'm sorry if I smell bad like that."

Philip didn't need to have the words sung to him. He'd chanted them from the security of a group of friends many times. They had seemed funny then. Harmless re-enforcer's of the fact that we are here and you are there. Reassurances of a superiority that they never need fear losing. Nestled in Stump's arms and hearing them come out of this huge, hulking, warm and protective body, in an innocent childlike voice reduced them to the hurtful barbs they were. He had made hundreds of confessions in the years since his First Holy Communion. While making them he hadn't felt absolved, remorseful or repentant. It was easy to whisper nothings behind a curtain to a man who wasn't listening, and accept the rote punishment of reciting more nothings to a God, who unfortunately heard everything. In the dark storm sheltered by the one you had offended a true confession hurt on its difficult way out and actually did seek forgiveness.

"I'm one uh them that used tuh sing that, I'm sorry an I ain't ever gonna do it again, or anything else that's mean tuh you, an I'll tell them other kids tuh shut up if they pick on you."

"Ok."

If he had laid all the Acts of Contrition, Hail Mary's and Our Fathers he had ever rushed through together in a line he wouldn't have felt this absolved. In spite of their perilous surroundings he felt better than he had for a long time. It hadn't dawned on him yet that unlike confessing to his church, this forgiveness came with strings of changed behavior attached.

They sat low, hunkered down and wind free, talking about things that they thought the other one would find interesting, and worrying quietly about whether or not Sam could ever find them. Philip shared stories of his family and many things he had overheard about town gossip, which his mother had in code like fashion passed on to his father. Stump told him bar stories and even some of what had happened to him in the state hospital.

"If we had uh fire it'd be perty nice sittin, an maybe Sam could see it an come get us." Philip was going to add that he was good at starting fires, but still thought that might be a sore subject with Stump, and decided to leave that part out.

The loose dead bark of the oak tree peeled off in huge pieces, and from Stump's pockets they had a selection of somewhat used napkins, and crumpled cigarette packages to help ignite the tinder. In just a few minutes there shelter was illuminated. Philip now sat on the bench like limb and fed the fire pieces of bark, and the broken up branches, which Stump gathered from the storm downed tree. The enthusiastic boy soon had a good sized blaze throwing off heat to their side facing the flames. Brought back to the level of understanding of early humans worshiping in front of a gift from lightening, but instead of praying for strips of mastodon flesh to roast on their fire, they wished for hamburgers, endless plates of home cooked food and bowls filled with "tator soup". It was contagious, the more they dwelled on what they wanted, the hungrier they became.

It was the boy's first experience with the kind of hunger that comes from even a few meals missed. Stump had been a week without a solid meal, but periodically in his life he would miss meals either through his own oversight, or before Ray had set up payments to the restaurants he frequented by running out of money to pay for food. By the time Sam found them hands outstretched to the flames, Philip was claiming he could eat a plate full of peas and buttered beets without a word of complaint.

"You got any uh that food, or yuh just tryin to torture yourselves to the point uh turnin cannibal?" Sam had approached them with his flashlight out. Several hundred yards away he had topped a slight rise along the side of the hill and had looked up from studying the ground with his steadily shrinking ray. He loudly thanked God and his eyes filled with tears, even at this distance in the snowy night the bonfire Stump and Philip had built could guide him through the woods. The painfully frustrating work of looking for tracks and following false leads was over. Several times he had thought of turning back for help. Not wanting to face a heart broken mother with the news that he had found her boy only to lose him to the night kept him going, just a little further. When he realized that his flashlight was about gone, and he had looked up to see the glow of the fire, he was once again wrestling with the thought. The distance to their windfall had taken several minutes, but after the tedium of tracking in the dark, it had seemed like flying over the ground on feet that disappeared somewhere in the dark down below, and the fire his eyes were riveted to drew nearer.

"Yer gonna have to carry the boy some more so I can work the light. Even if yuh have to step on the backs of my boots stay close, we ain't got enough battery left tuh do another jaunt like that."

Philip watched his fire gradually diminish in the distance, when they topped the rise and started down the other side it turned into a vague glow and then the snow and the dark consumed even that.

Chapter 25

Mr. Anderman had answered three phone calls assuring the callers they would check in the places suggested when either the boys or his wife returned. Each time it rang he rushed to answer hoping it would be an apologetic Philip, with some far fetched excuse for being gone. In between calls he looked out the window at the street light shaking in the wind. It's swatch of light filled with a constant parade of hard driven snow. A week ago he had hoped for snow to aid in the upcoming deer season, now he cursed every punishing flake that fell. He walked to the door and opened it to the cold air of the porch. Reaching out his hand felt around in the dark and finally found and flicked on the light above the front step. Closing the door he went back to his chair by the window. All day long he had sat in the woods, his imagination turning exposed rocks and tree trunks into bedded down deer. He had stared at one rock so long he could see the nose, ears, and eventually by craning his neck to the right just a bit he could see a good sized rack of horns. Every year stories were told of people taking shots at such apparitions, Mr. Anderman new better, even so when he stretched his legs at noon he kept his eyes on the rock and his rifle at the ready. Ears and nose turned into patches of lichen and the horns, a bush growing a few feet behind the rock. Standing gave a new perspective, still all afternoon when his eyes passed over the spot in their constant search for game he would see, momentarily, a buck staring back at him. He studied the snowy yard and as far down the avenue as the street light lit with the same intensity, but the images his brain conjured weren't of successful ends to his hunting, it was dark now.

Finally his stomach reminded him that a summer sausage sandwich six hours ago wasn't adequate fodder, his mind left its pointless and painful crusade through all the things that could have happened, and he focused on getting something ready for the searchers to eat when they returned.

The bucket under the sink held an assortment of wrinkled up potatoes, their white whiskers seeking nonexistent sunlight. He took them to the porch and dumped them out in the garbage. His frugal wife insisted on using even the last of the spuds, he hated peeling the soft, pruney tubers when he knew that several hundred pounds of nice smooth ones were sacked up in a cool corner of the basement. He went down the stairs, head held low, almost to his shoulder, to avoid contact with the low wooden beams. When he reached the bottom step the phone started ringing. He turned and rushed back up the steps bumping his head on the first timber, still cursing softly and rubbing his forehead he picked the phone up on the fourth ring.

"Hello Anderman's"

A soft girl's voice responded, "Is Tom there?"

"This is Tom."

"I'm sorry. It didn't sound like you. Last night yuh said yuh'd call, don't yuh love me now?"

"Oh you must uh wanted my son Tom, he's out lookin for his little brother." He would have asked for her name, but he heard a startled gasp and a click on the other end. On any other night he would have played the game a little longer. He felt Tom the younger needed occasional buckets of water thrown on his relationships. And senior didn't need to have some girl calling every ten minutes to see if junior was home, but just not following through on promises.

Back down in the basement he picked out a bucket full of the bigger potatoes, rubbing the now dry earth off of them and into the burlap sack with his hands. He selected a somewhat misshapen Harralsons apple from the bushel basket under the steps and started taking big crisp bites from it as he ascended the stairs. He sat the bucket down by the sink, fished the soaking deer organs out of the red tinged water, and squeezed them lightly to extract a little more blood before sitting them down on the rubber mat the dish rack usually rested on. Pulling the plug sent a gory whirlpool down the drain. He dumped his potatoes in the sink and washed the remainder of the dirt from their light brown skins. The potatoes and a gallon or so of water went into the big soup kettle and onto the big burner of the gas range with the maximum flame licking its blackened bottom. He put the lid on the kettle, the bucket back under the sink, and sat down to a cigarette and more staring out the window into the snow.

The telephone rang again. "Hello."

"Hi Dad did he show up yet?"

"No. Where you at?"

"Down at the Shell station. We checked down by the tracks and in the swamp. We asked in all the bars and restaurants thinkin maybe some hunters might uh seen him but nobody has. Were goin up to the hill behind the school, kids sometimes slide back there, an maybe he hit a tree or sumpthin."

"Yuh do that an then just come home, we'll eat an try to figger out some sort'a plan."

There were no words of encouragement left, no maybe he's visiting so and so, something was terribly wrong and they both knew it. He hooked the ear piece of the phone in its cradle and picked up the tiny tin horn from the window sill. Out on front step he let out a shrill blast and stood in the pool of light from the bulb above his head. Pat the Labrador from next door gave his mandatory coon dog like howl in response, and the snow whipped by in the biting wind.

Chapter 26

Fred had tried to get his mother to talk several times. He told her every breath taking moment of his triumph over the, "perty big for a fawn", and had even injected some of the departures from the truth he had been saving for Tuesday after Deer Day at school. Nothing drew her out of her silent determined driving. He turned his head to the window and looked out at the empty streets. The plows wouldn't be out until the snow quit falling and in places drifts slowed them down. To Fred this was just another example of one of his brothers stealing what should have been his moment. To get a deer on the first day ever of hunting was a big deal, he felt cheated of the basking he should have been doing right now. His fawn should have been hanging from one of the hooks in the ceiling of the cold porch, where he could have gone out to check it, to feel it's side to reaffirm that it was still there and not just a dream. Instead his precious deer lay in the back of the pickup getting covered by the snow, while he drove around in the dark looking for his dumb little brother. Every time something good happened to him something better happened to one of his brothers. Along with these feelings of bitterness there was a flood of ideas of ways he could come up with the one place no one else had thought to look, where Philip was laying in need of help, and he would find him, to be placed back in the center of an adoring family. Back where he belonged. He also had some minor feelings of concern for his younger brother but not many. He was young enough to still believe that bad things always seemed to happen somewhere else, and just couldn't happen to anyone he knew, especially not to anyone in his family.

The town police car was parked on the side street between Eikilson's Grocery, and Closed for Season 1896 Ice Cream Parlor. Mrs. Anderman eased her Chevrolet through the ridge of untracked snow and pulled up behind the officer.

"You stay here. I'm gonna ask him if anybody's seen Philip, maybe someone called in since we been drivin."

"Be careful Ma, if yuh wake him up yuh might get shot."

"Don't talk smart about policemen there out here helpin us when we need em."

She stepped out of their vehicle and approached the patrol car through the deep snow. Fred watched the silhouette of "Art the cop" as his mother knocked on the window. Art disappointed him by simply turning towards the window and rolling it down. He had heard boys whose parents let them go out at night talk about tossing fire crackers under Art's car, and running away from the rudely awakened officer. It was a source of occasional entertainment to the town youngsters. They didn't pay attention to the constant battle between Art and the city council over the need for more than summer backups for their chief of police. So he slept and they saved money. The town cradled in the safety of seasonal remoteness managed to remain nearly crime free. His mother talked for a short time and then turned back to her car.

"He seen anything?"

"No! Says the Sheriff called an asked if he's seen Philip, but he hasn't. He said he'd keep his eyes out for him." She didn't add that she had suggested even keeping his eyes open for her boy would be appreciated, and that driving around looking for him was more important then his ambush for speeding out of town deer hunters.

"I was thinkin maybe he went slidin up at the school, an hit his head. Lot's uh times kids take uh chunk uh cardboard up there an slide on it." He could picture Philip lying partially covered by a snow bank with maybe just his arm sticking out. Fred even had the likely tree on the hill picked out where he would reclaim his glory for the day, and find his missing brother.

"Are there many trees on them hills?"

Fred knowing his Mothers infinite memory for anything remotely exciting that could pose a danger for her children, answered cautiously. "Well not if yer careful an pick the safe hills, but a kid like Philip, yuh just never know."

"That's uh good idea Fred, we haven't checked the streets up that way yet anyhow. I don't want you boys sliding up there if there's trees. Plenty uh hills in your own neighborhood with no trees to get hurt on."

Fred silently stewed over the position his younger brother had placed him in. He no longer could respond to his Mother's question about where he had been on winter days with the non-descriptive reply of "slidin", without her automatically asking "where at", and then he might be forced to lie. The monumental unfairness of the evening seemed to have no light side. Fred resigned himself to silent brooding and stared out the window at the hard world.

Parked on the side street it seemed that the snow had let up a little. When they turned out onto the highway, and started driving towards the turn to the school, their speed and the street lights made it seem that they were sitting still with a shifting wall of white moving by. Occasional openings gave them brief glimpses at darkened store fronts which were familiar, but the snow would swallow them up and in the next letup something else had appeared. Trying to find something as big and as immobile as a road in the storm was proving to be a difficult task. Finding Philip in this weather by driving around was like hoping to track the movement of a speck of dust in a cardboard kaleidoscope. Mrs. Anderman had started the search with a need to do something other than wait by the telephone and look out the window. She wasn't giving up, but she needed to get her family together again, to regroup, and assure herself that they hadn't overlooked something. Out of the snow the Shell Station materialized. She plowed through the ridge of snow created by the passing of other cars, and started up the hill to the school.

"We're gonna look here an then go home an see if the boys found out anything. Somebody probly called by now an we'll find out he's been locked in their cellar or sumpthin nutty like that."

They were nearing the midpoint of the hill when a ridge of snow deposited by the wind brought them to a stop. Mrs. Anderman miraculously managed to back most of the way down the slope, and a little into a driveway, before the rear half of her car became firmly wedged in a snow drift. She tried driving back and forth to pack down a trail to drive out on, and though her tires turned obediently, the frame of the car was so stuck that the spinning treads whined ineffectively above the small sheets of ice each had created.

"Shit!"

Fred looked at his mother in utter amazement. Although he had heard adults swear, (especially his father whenever he was forced to do plumbing repairs to their aging house), he would have sworn that that word would never fall from her lips, even if she were hit in the face with a shovel full of the same.

"I'll get out an push." His mother was silent, but Fred was sure that what he was seeing in the glow from the dashboard were tears glistening on her cheeks. He pushed open the door, plowing back snow which was piled at least a quarter of the way up its side, and stepped out into the storm.

Fred had hoped and prayed for many things, always for things. Standing in the wind driven snow he offered up his first request for something. If his brother could be found safe he knew his mother would be happy again. In the way his religion had taught him he bartered, safe brother, pure life, a simple offer he was willing at that point in time to honor. He pushed with all his skinny might and the car sat solidly in the snow bank, its tires singing a high pitched song. The anger, fear and frustration of the night exploded within him. He swore ferociously into the howling wind in the words his father had given him. The vexation at a stupid little brother causing his mother to swear and cry, fury at the snow for catching them, and covering his deer.

Stuck in the drift beside the driveway, its handle still visible above the accumulation of snow, a grain scoop left by it's owner in anticipation of storms to come. Fred grabbed it up and attacked the imprisoning drift with astonishing energy. A steady stream of obscenities poured from his mouth in direct violation of the pure life he had only seconds before promised and mixed with the shovels full of snow he threw up into the whipping wind. He shoveled and pushed and then shoveled more, driven on by the picture of his mother illuminated by instrument lights. And then he was done. It was like he was empty and very tired. He walked between the wall of snow he had hacked out of the drift and the side of his mother's car, and knocked on her side window. She rolled it down a bit.

"Put it into drive when I bang on the trunk, I think it's all shoveled free towards the street now." He walked to the back of the car, shoved the borrowed scoop back into the drift, and positioned himself to the mid rear area of the car. When he felt that his feet were anchored solidly enough to push he hammered on the trunk with his mitten'd hand. The Chevrolet surged forward effortlessly and Fred gave a mighty heave and landed face first in the snow well behind the now free automobile. He scrambled to his feet and ran to catch up to his mother. She finally stopped when the car was well onto the street. Fred opened the door and slid onto the seat. The heat from the blower felt like a match held to his cheeks.

"You did real good Fred, I'm sorry I swore, I just couldn't take any more with gettin stuck after everything else today."

Not knowing why Fred reached over and patted her gloved hand, but said nothing.

"I think we should just skip checking on them sliding hills for now. Maybe we better just go home, and if we have to go out again we'll take the truck." She released the brake and started driving down the hill and towards home when suddenly someone pounded on the trunk. Mrs. Anderman stopped the car and turned her head in time to see Frank and Tom open the rear doors of the car and climb in.

"Where the heck did you two come from?"

"We were thinkin maybe Philip could uh been slidin up on the school house hill, but the Fisher kids were up there an said they'd been there all day an hadn't seen him. We looked everywhere, even checked all the cafes and bars to see if any one saw him, nobody's seen nothin. I called Dad an told him what we'd done an that we would check up here, so when we didn't find nothin up there we started headin home. This heat feels so good, I figgered for sure we would have a long walk with that wind hittin us."

"We couldn't get up the hill and then I got stuck. We would uh still been sittin there if Fred hadn't shoveled us out."

"Yea we were up wind from him an could hear him talkin over his strategy. If he wouldn't uh worked so fast we would uh helped out."

Fred looked over the seat at the dark shapes of his brothers. He stared at them trying to see if they would in some way signal how much they had heard. He decided that whatever they had heard he would have to hope they could keep to themselves.

Chapter 27

The beam from Sam's flashlight was just a feeble yellow hole in the storm. It ended short of the length of his stride, and every time he stopped to assure himself that he was staying true to the trail, Stump, who didn't have the benefit of its pale illumination, would nearly knock him down from behind. When they were still in the woods and hadn't made it to the old road, he had stopped to make sure that Stump and Philip were still with him. He had called out and didn't receive a response. By yelling and flashing his light in a circle around him into the darkness he was finally rewarded with the high pitched voice of the boy screaming something unintelligible from the direction of the cedar swamp. After they regrouped Sam took the rope he used for dragging deer out of the woods from the game pouch in the back of his hunting coat and tied one end around his waist and the other around Stump. In this manner they had stayed together in the darkness and the snow. Though the occasional collision was inevitable it at least let him know where his two charges were.

The slope of the trail had been fairly easy to follow and Sam had been able to take them ten steps in total dark, flash on his light, and then go ten more steps with it off. With this calculated risk he saved some battery for the place at the top of the hill where the road went crooked and the sumac brush took over. They were near the top but not to the sumacs, but his tracks were gone. Maybe a fresh set of batteries would have revealed where he was, but he didn't have a fresh set of batteries. In the area of his brain that was unclouded with fact and reasoning, the place that told him when to turn left at night to avoid stubbing his toe on the way to see why his boy was fussing, he felt they were still on the trail. Unfortunately this instinct wasn't always right. Sometimes he stubbed his toe in the dark, sometimes in the middle of a cloudy day, trusting his instinct, he could get turned around in the woods and have to dig out his compass to find the way home. Not always, but often enough that squatting here on his heels, in the middle of the night, in a blizzard, simply feeling that they were headed in the right direction wasn't all that comforting.

He turned off the flashlight while he thought. They were near the top of the hill, he could tell that by the bitter force of the wind on his cheeks. Without the shelter of the natural slope of the land the snow would fill in his tracks faster, and that would explain why ten steps back he had readable sign that was gone now. It was also possible that he had gone to the side. With the wind like this, even if you tried not to, the natural thing to do was to turn your face a little to the side, to protect it, like turning away from a slap to the face. He had noticed earlier, before he had found Stump and the boy sitting by their fire, that if he turned the flashlight off and adjusted to the darkness, and then flicked it back on, his eyes would pick up a depression in the snow that they had missed before. He pushed the button forward. At first he thought that with his mitten'd hand he had somehow failed to engage the switch. He tried it again with it held up to his ear and could hear the clicking noise. By pointing it into his eyes he could see a faint glow where the wires in the bulb came close together, but then even that was gone. For some reason he clicked the on-off switch back to the off position, and tucked it into his game pouch.

By now Rita would be worried. She would call his mother again to see if there was some reason not to, but a full fledged anxiety attack was in order when someone didn't come home on time during a storm like this. Maybe she would call the Sheriff and report him missing, but on opening night of deer season, and with a storm, they wouldn't exactly be calling out the National Guard to look for him. With his hands free of holding the flashlight, he covered his face and tried to warm his cheeks. Even with the thick mittens held to them he couldn't tell if they were covered. Frostbite reminded him of Korea, that and again having people's lives dependent on his decisions. If he would have known this storm was coming he would have stayed in Albert's shack, better for the Anderman's to spend a night worrying then to risk everything in a blizzard. He hated "if only's", they occupied a portion of his brain he needed now.

An idea came to him, and although it was a time consuming way of going forward it was all he had.

"Stump, you an Philip need to stick yer arms out to yer sides, away from yer bodies. We're gonna work side to side with the wind in are faces. When yuh feel brush yell out an then we'll work to the other side. Once we feel where the edges are we'll guess at the middle an go forward ten steps."

"What'll we do then?"

Sam looked in the direction of Stump's voice. "Then we'll do it all over again till we get outta here."

Stump shrugged his shoulders to the unseeing Sam, and the trio started groping their way through the night.

Philip was the first to call out when a low hanging branch stabbed him in the ear. Sam reached around a little more and felt enough brush to feel they were on the edge of the trail. They then moved to the right until Sam struck a tree trunk with his waving arm. The group then took half as many steps back to the left as they had taken to find the other side of what they prayed was the trail, and then took ten long strides as straight into the wind as they could manage. Through the storm they moved forward in this slow, sometimes painful manner, with all of them encountering poking sticks as often with their unprotected faces as they did with outstretched hands. After what seemed an eternity of this torture. They had brush to the front of them as well as to their sides.

"This is gotta be the sumacs, If it ain't were gonna haf'ta try to get another fire goin an then just sit it out. Stump, you hold Philip up as high as yuh can. Look forward into the wind kid. Can yuh see anything?"

After what seemed forever Philip replied. "It's like there's some kind'a lights over there or maybe sumpthin glowin."

"Is it straight into the wind?"

"No. More over to the right."

Sam tried not to feel elated. He would save that emotion until they were sitting in a warm pickup with the engine running and the snow blowing harmlessly by. The truck lights should have been to the left, but with the blind groping they had just finished doing he felt overwhelmingly blessed that they were any where near to the trail. He started walking to the right using both arms as shields to fend off the branches which seemed to want to poke out his eyes, when suddenly his rope tether brought him to an unexpected and abrupt halt. He pulled on it several times before he heard the noise of Philip's voice above the wind. He turned and returned to his anchor.

Stump had made only three steps in tow of Sam when Philip realized he had made a mistake. He knew right from left but every once in a while they would get turned around on him. It was embarrassing but he knew he must stop Sam before they were lost again, reluctantly he was forced to say. "Stop him Stump. Them lights are the other way. To the left, I get em mixed up sometimes."

Stump had replied. "I member cuz I cut uh big chunk outta my right thumb when Ma got mad at me for choppin sticks with her hatchet. Now I just member right's the thumb that got sore an left's the other one."

"Why'd yuh stop?"

"I got my rights and lefts mixed up. I'm sorry."

"No sweat kid. Yuh must uh meant yer other right. I know some grownups that would uh waited till the next time we checked to tell me I wandered too far right an made it out my fault, stead uh just sayin they screwed up." Sam paused a second. "Lift him up one more time Stump, to make sure we get goin right, or maybe I mean left."

Philip figured the last part was a joke, and liked the way he had made him feel getting turned around wasn't stupid, and admitting it, was somehow a mark of being smart. Stump hoisted him up into the air where the wind could hit him square in the face all the way from Western Canada. He looked at the glowing area to the left until the bite of the storm hurt his eyes. "It's uh car or sumpthin cuz I can see two headlights, an it's just uh little bit left of the way the winds blowin."

Two lifts later to check their bearings and even Sam was sure he could see an aura of light in the blowing snow. Once they had cleared the sumacs, with the remainder of the trail lighted, it seemed like they were running, all the snow flakes illuminated in the headlights rushed by them on the wind as they hurried forward.

The inside of the pickup felt hot after what they had been through. The snow landing on the windshield melted and slid to the bottom reforming as sludgy ice. Sam not wanting to go out in the cold again turned the knob for the wipers and was rewarded with a steady, cleaning flop. He shifted into reverse and eased out the clutch. The rear tires moved them back a few feet, but then started spinning. He pulled forward and backed up again. This time he made it back almost to the county road before coming to a halt. He tried pulling forward again but didn't make any progress as he backed up.

"I hate to do this to yuh Stump, but I need some weight over them back tires. I need yuh to get out an get into the back end an sit back by the tailgate. I'll pull us forward an yer weight will get us right out."

Without a word Stump slipped back out into the cold. In the warmth of the cab Sam and Philip felt the rear end of the pickup sag as Stump climbed over the edge and sat down. Sam went forward as before, but with Stump over the rear tires for traction they easily made it over the plow ridge from the snow from Monday. Sam leaned across the seat and reached past Philip to open the door for Stump.

"It ain't over yet, but we sure had uh hell of uh trip so far boys." Sam looked out the window at the snow filled road. He hoped not to have to send Stump out as dead weight over the rear axle again, but the view ahead of him made him feel it was likely that he would.

Chapter 28

Mr. Anderman was relieved to see the two older boys climb out of the back of the Chevrolet and join his wife and Fred as they trudged through the snow towards their house. He had prayed silently for a third figure to exit the back of the car, but was glad to have at least these four out of the storm. He had the potato's scalded skins peeled off. The heart and liver were sliced up and dredged in flour, ready to fry with chunks of onions in bacon grease from the morning's breakfast.

The door squeaked out on the porch and he tried to smile reassuringly as they entered the house. "I got some stuff ready to cook here. I figgered we should eat before goin out again."

"You'll have to take the pickup the snows too deep an we kept draggin. We nearly got stuck uh couple times and it seems to be gettin worse, not letting up at all." No one asked if there was any news. Their father's face spoke of the emptiness, and to make conversation about their fears would do no good.

"If were gonna take the truck you boys go get Fred's deer outta the back an hang it up in the porch, then yuh can get on some dry clothes."

Fred brightened at mention of his fawn. "Do we gotta skin it Dad? I'd like Philip to see it with the hide on."

Mr. Anderman smiled they needed some positive thinking just now. "Nea, I spose it's frozen harder than hammered owl shit by now anyway. Just hang it up, an tomorrow after Philip gets uh look, we'll build uh fire in the barrel stove an try thawing it out enough to peel the hair off."

Fred grinning led the threesome back out into the blizzard. "You think he's ok don'tcha, probly just screwin round like Ma said an got locked up in some basement or sumpthin dumb like he's all the time doin."

Tom looked down at his brother. "Yea probly fell asleep readin comic books in the drug store an got locked in." Then with obviously feigned sincerity he added. "Gee Frank don'tcha think Pa should uh left this awesome carcass layin back here for some extra weight, yuh know for traction."

Frank who had one of the deer's legs in hand and was dragging it out onto the snow laughed. "Shit! He probly figgered it'd blow out in all this wind."

Tom and Frank stood beside the dead animal and Fred thought they were about to start dragging it down the trail to the porch when Tom turned to him. "It ain't my deer. I might help hoist it up on the hook, but you gotta drag it in. I'm through haulin it round, while you make moony eyes at it, an figger out lies to tell everyone at school bout what uh mighty hunter you are."

Fred picked the rope up that was tied around its neck and pulled the fawn towards their house. On the foot packed trail the little deer slid easily.

Frank stepped out ahead of his brothers. "I'm gonna put some newspapers down so Ma don't have uh shit fit if it bleeds any on her linoleum."

By the time they reached the porch Frank had the light in the porch on and was spreading out pages of the local paper beneath three hooks which were screwed into the wooden rafters of the porch. They picked the deer up and carried it into the porch, and laid it down on the papers.

Tom pulled a step ladder over to the front hook, and then squatted down by the hind legs of the deer. He pulled out his knife and made a slit in the thin layer of skin between leg bone and the large tendon by its hoof. He then threaded a short piece of rope through the hole he had just cut and through a similar hole in the opposing leg which already had a metal registration tag stuck through it. With a simple knot he secured both ends of the rope to the fawn's legs. "Frank you climb up there an Fred an me will hoist it up. I'd say to wait till its hooves hit the ceiling but we'd have to use a ladder to skin it if we lifted this poor little shit that high up."

With an easy lift the deer was hanging from the hook and a minute later Frank had wedged a piece of board between its hams to pry the hind quarters apart. A shorter stick was stuck between the left and right ribs. They hadn't had any lectures on how to do this, what they did, was what they had seen on many fall days. A tradition passed on by interested watching and the unspoken knowledge that to live is to eat, and to eat is to kill, or to have someone do the killing for you. Inside of all three was the gnawing concern for their younger brother, but this was something that had to be done too.

When they were done they went to the door into the house. Frank was going to turn off the light when Fred stopped him. "Don't. I wanna look at him for a while." Tom and Frank left him alone on the porch and he walked back to where the fawn hung. Tiny drops of blood were dripping off the end of its downward hanging nose. He rubbed the tiny nubbins on its forehead wishing they would have been spikes or even forked horns. He felt bad and he didn't understand it. Every season he had watched his brothers leave and wished that he could go along. Next year he knew he would be just as excited and would pull the trigger as he had earlier in the day, but looking at the hide covered meat hanging here, it was somehow painful. So he squatted there rubbing the deer's head trying to remember just how it had happened. From the second he first heard its feet crunching the thin crust on the snow, to the first glimpse of dark brown moving through the distant brush. He tried to erase all of his concoctions so what he saw was true. From the feeling of his heart about to pound right through his chest to the sudden thought that he was supposed to bring his shotgun up and shoot. He didn't want it all to be a blur. He wanted a mental snapshot of each instant to examine out of respect for the moment and to see why he should feel such a mixture of elation and sorrow. He decided it had to be because of Philip being gone. Maybe this had not only pushed his accomplishment out of everyone else's focus, but bumped it out of his own as well. He knew it was some of that, but from the instant he had pulled the trigger he also knew that there was no taking it back. The act was irretrievable, permanent, the ending of something he had no power to create. He knew that the only way to come close to making it right was to remember it this way, and to make sure that none of the animal went to waste.

In the house Tom and Frank were taking off layers of hunting clothes upstairs in their room. Mrs. Anderman was looking out the window, silently tearing herself apart for things she could have done, things that she would have never done. Her husband stood by the stove searing a dinner no one had the appetite for. The telephone rang and she reached up and answered "Anderman's. No. No word at all." She hung up without a "thanks for calling" or even a "goodbye". Her eyes went back to the steady sweep of snow past their window. A pickup nearly as disreputable as their own pulled up behind her Chevrolet.

"Some one in uh pickup is here Tom, they turned off their lights." She felt a rush of excitement surely this must be someone who had found Philip. Two adult sized people exited the vehicle. Well at least it could be someone with news of her boy. In the snow she couldn't make out who it was, but they were walking down the path to her house. A sinking thought caught her in the chest as she suddenly realized it was just some of Tom's hunting friends coming to talk over the day. The man in the lead was still wearing his red hunting clothes. She sat back in the chair in despair.

Tom looked out the window over her shoulder. "Wonder who the hell that could be out on uh night like this?"

Fred was shaken from his reverie by someone pounding on the porch door. He went to it quickly and opened it to a blast of frigid air carrying hard flakes of snow. He had seen the man filling the doorway, but hadn't a clue as to what he would be doing knocking on their door. The man pushed on by him and an even stranger sight followed. Sitting high in the second man's arms was Philip.

Mr. Anderman had thoughts similar to his wife's. He decided it was some of his friends from work that had spent too much time drinking in celebration of a big buck, and had decided to go out bragging. He went to the door determined to send them on their way with as brief an explanation as he could get by with.

Fred opened the door before his father had a chance. Sam Cloud came in with Stump as big as the doorway following. Philip looked down at his parents not knowing what to expect. They were silent trying to come up with thought or words to associate with what they saw.

Sam realizing how strange this must appear broke the silence. "Hi Tom, suppose you been wonderin where this ones been all day."

Philip decided it was time to speak. "I'm awful sorry Ma I lost my new boot."

Stump stooped over and deposited the one booted boy on the floor, and then tried to disappear into the corner where the jackets hung.

"Well I'll be damned. Where did he? Thanks Sam. I don't have a clue what the hells goin on here but thanks. Thanks so much. How?" He couldn't go on. He stood and watched as Philip ran to his wife's open arms and hugged her.

Tom and Frank hearing the disturbance came running down the stairs and stopped frozen in mid step and mid thought by the odd grouping in their kitchen.

Sam looked at the stricken Stump and knew it was up to him to speak of what had happened during the day, but he had something to do first. "Can I use yer phone, my wife is probly worried sick. I was sposed to be home hours ago."

"God yea, go ahead."

Sam went to the telephone and dialed quickly. "Hi! No I'm just fine. That'll take bout an hour to tell yuh all uh that, too much happened. Yea he was there. Got him with me right now. At Tom Anderman's. It's uh long story. Yea I know yuh do. I'll be home in just uh little bit, I gotta take Stump to his place then I'll be right home. Yea me too, Bye."

During his conversation everyone had wanted to appear not to be listening so there eyes had gone to Stump who appeared truly miserable. He stood on one leg and tried to rap the ice build up out of his disintegrating boot.

With Sam off the telephone questioning eyes turned back to him. "I wasn't there for most of it but this is what Stump and Philip and Alfred said." He then went into the story he had gathered from the three in Alfred's shack, and on to their dangerous journey through the storm. Philip interjected here and there to clear up minor misunderstandings, but Stump stood silently working at his boot sole.

During the recounting of their adventures Mrs. Anderman frequently looked down at Philip as if to make sure he was still there. She was torn between joy at his return and concern over his disobedience. She got up mid point and went to finish the dinner that had nearly burned on the stove. When Sam was done she extended her hand. "I know we never met but I'm Ruth, an I want yuh to know I'm just so thankful for what you an Carl did. Now Carl I know I should uh been doin more than just sayin Hi to you on the streets all these years. Yer Mom and Dad were good neighbors for so many years. You saved my little boy's life just as sure as there's uh God he would uh drowned out there an no one would uh ever found him. I am so grateful. You can never know how grateful." She was crying again, but she had her youngest by her side and her fingers entangled in his hair in an affectionate way, at least for that minute. "Yuh gotta stay for supper it's the least I can do. An I wanna look at that icy foot yuh got there. Uh person could lose toes with uh foot like that. Sam I know yuh gotta get home, but if there's anything we can ever do just say the word. Don't you worry we'll get Carl home to the hotel, but I'm gonna look after him uh little bit first."

Sam saw the wisdom of this. He had noticed Stump's foot while he had talked to his wife. His cheeks felt funny with frost bite. He could only imagine how that foot must feel. "I better get goin. The way these roads are I might end up stuck again before I get home."

Stump looked pleadingly at him. "Maybe I otta ride with yuh case yuh need me to sit in the back in deep snow."

Sam looked sympathetically at him, but knew that right now he needed to get his foot cared for, and he didn't think anyone at the hotel would do it. Besides Stump deserved a little mothering, even if he didn't want it. "Nea I'll be just fine. You did good today Stump, I mean, Carl you did real good. Eat lot's uh that heart an liver an them potatoes. The way he's been starvin out there with Alfred yuh better cut uh hind quarter off uh that fawn an fry it up too."

With Sam gone Stump felt too much the center of attention. Everyone was staring at him, he smiled submissively, his eyes suddenly needed to study the end of his bad boot, and his finger wandered to his nose. Everyone looked away.

Chapter 29

Far away in the darkness the Ring Billed Duck swam through the storm. The size of its opening in the ice had been reduced to a few precious yards, and even that had a thin film of crystals and matted snow. He struggled to keep them from entrapping him. When the boy who threw the stones had broken through the ice he'd had much more room. Enough to dive and feed from the bottom. He wouldn't be able to feed anymore. He hadn't felt anger towards the boy for disturbing him with the rocks or sorrow for the predicament when the boy disappeared under the ice. Nor had he experienced any emotions when the bigger one came along and snatched the boy from the water. In the way of birds he had observed and accepted both the tragedy and resurrection. He feared the slowly encircling death that awaited him, but his webbed feet churned behind him at the same pace they had ever since he had broken out of his egg shell three summers ago. Deliberately, forcefully, yet calmly he kicked and pulled his feet alternately away and back towards his down covered belly.

He was a fully mature duck so he had seen and smelled death many times and knew a month ago that it was coming for him. The man that time had jumped up from the cattails and startled him and the group that had formed around him as summer ended into a tight indecisive group in the middle of the pond. The man had shot at them in an attempt to get them to fly, hoping some would swing into range of his shotgun. Many of the those hatched that year did. He had waited as experience had taught him and flown out in the confusion of death as the young were knocked out of the sky. He was nearly clear of the Bass Wood trees ringing the slough when the man took one last desperation shot. He felt the lead pellet breaking the bone of his wing at the same time that he heard the final shot. With one wing still intact he careened into the thick cattails and lily pads on the end of the lake furthest away from danger. He had lain there perfectly still while the man made his dog search out the dead and wounded. The lily pads flopping in the breeze had protected him then. Giving cover to his form, and the wind which stirred them carried his scent away from the pursuers. Escaping the sudden death which would have come from the man ringing his neck if the brown dog had found him might have been better then this slow end in the darkness. But just as the matter with the boy had been observed with detachment so were the last hours of his life. A human faced with this horror could have sworn at his murders and cursed God for abandonment. The duck swam on.

After the man departed he had swum out to the middle of the pond and tried to flap his wings. The right one was strong, but even stretched out to its full length it could only slap the water ineffectively without the support of its mate. The left wing was broken out near its first joint, where it elbowed. If the break would have been above this spot the duck could have flown in short spurts to save itself from the foxes and mink that were sure to be coming for him. Broken in between the joint and his body the Wing was worthless. Two days after the injury another group of Ring Bills flew in and fed in the pond for several days. Before being shot he had been a dominant duck, a duck that chased other ducks out of his way when he wanted to. Now he was even less then the immature or the very old making their last migration. The young could chase and pick at his backside if he was seen with a snail or a bit of weed they wanted. By the time they flew away he had taken to segregating himself and watched their departure as he had the boy's near drowning. They leapt into the air and swung several times around the little pond until they could turn south to fly towards the sun. All through the fall migrating ducks had come and gone. Ten Wood Ducks had stayed until the hunter came and shot two of the beautiful drakes. They had not tormented him or chased him away from the good feeding spots. He had swam with them and since he wasn't one of them hadn't been seen as a threat to any ones place in dominance. When the hunter came he dove under the water and swam to the opposing shore and crawled up to hide in the weeds.

Occasionally through the Autumn he would try the damaged wing and though it grew strong enough to help him flop away from a fox that caught him too close to shore, it never would support him in a flight of more than forty yards. The fox had splashed after him and then turned away empty mouthed as if it really hadn't wanted duck anyway. The duck had taken to sleeping in the middle of the pond after that.

When the water near shore started to freeze several days earlier his attempts at flight became more serious. The groups of ducks as they woke up in the morning would un-tuck their heads from beneath their wings and could feel the urgency in the air, a strong need to be on their way. They would feed on the snails and minnows and then in unison explode from the water. The duck would flop unproductively around the surface of the slough in an attempt to follow and then drop back into the water. Feeling the same urgent need but unable to meet it.

The ice in front of him refused to part. His ever diminishing circles had turned into a short narrow channel and it was getting shorter with each trip. He turned by partially climbing out onto the ice, facing into the wind driven biting snow, and down the length of his channel, he started flopping his wings and running with his webbed feet slapping down on the slushy water, pounding his wings not feeling the pain. He was once again in the air being lifted on the wind with his wings sending him higher up into the night and snow.

Above the snow it was calm and bright. He turned towards the light and flew by the reckoning of a thousand memories.

Chapter 30

The stars were shot across the sky so thick that it was light even without a moon. Stump walked the lonely streets looking in windows at families cleaning up the remains of their holiday feasts. It was cold, as it always seemed to be. All of the bars and restaurants were closed with the holidays. In the lonely darkness he could stop and see what the families were doing without fear of being seen. Some were playing games, others busy going after an extra desert, occasionally a dog would raise the alarm if he stood too long, causing him to go on to another glimpse into someone else's life.

He had stopped by the girl's house and looked in there half hoping to see her by the window looking out. He thought of her often and found little comfort in her being gone away and no longer a temptation. As much as it hurt seeing her sitting in bars, or leaving them with men, it was more painful not to see her at all. She wasn't home. The nasty faced father was there with his nose bristling hairs. Between him and the girl's mother stood a bottle of brandy. They weren't eating or playing any games that he could see, just sitting at an all but empty table, staring at each other.

Sam had seen him the other day and said he was going to his mother's house to be with her after they went to Brainerd to see his sister. He missed Sam especially in the summer when he was gone for so long.

The snow squeaked under his new insulated boots. He stuffed his hands deep into the pockets of his coat and walked some more to stay warm. He wondered what the old men who didn't have families to go visit were watching at the hotel. He hoped it wouldn't be boxing. He looked up at the stars. It stung his nose a little when he breathed, so no matter what they were watching he knew he should go back. He felt inside his pocket once again and fondled the large, still warm well wrapped parcel. Mrs. Anderman still made the most delicious rhubarb cake.

The End

Epilogue

The winter was unusually long even by Minnesota standards that year, and during what came to be known as the "Deer Opener Storm", five hunters and three stranded motorists froze to death.

As Sam had predicted Stump was a hero, for a while, especially while the frostbite on his foot healed and he was still limping. Eventually the limp went away and people stopped wanting to shake his hand and quit pointing at him. He liked slipping back into near anonymity. He was a regular visitor at the Anderman's after the events of the autumn.

Mrs. Eikilson's opinion of Stump didn't change a bit. She still thinks he's a nice boy and if he shows up in the afternoon, after she has had just a few highballs, to do an odd job for her, she gives him twice the money her husband promised.

Erma Schwartz had many opportunities for several weeks to remind everyone that she had always maintained that Stump had come from good blood, and blood would always tell.

Peggy Slayton was never seen again in town. Gossip had it that she was working the streets in Minneapolis. Later it was rumored that she was a nurses aide in an old folks home in Little Falls.

Mr. and Mrs. Slayton went on in their shared purgatory staying together out of spite, existing for the sole purpose of denying the other his or her share of their belongings.

Sam Cloud was hired by the same construction company that Tom Anderman worked for. He had to take a cut in his hourly pay compared to his job on the road, but not that big of a cut, and since it wasn't seasonal he actually made considerably more. Best of all he didn't have to travel anymore.

Tom Anderman shot a doe with horns that fall and a constant parade of visitors came by to see it. The other boys enjoyed the shared bragging rights.

Philip spent most of his non-school hours for several weeks at home imprisoned by his mothers sentence of being restricted to his yard.

Ray was happy to get Stump back from the unknown, but came to the same conclusion Sam had much earlier, that Alfred was better off in the woods. Too much good living could kill him off quicker than struggling with the elements for survival would, so he didn't try to talk him into moving back to the hotel.

Alfred came into town in late November and pawned a single shot twelve gauge to Leo for fifteen dollars. He tried to convince Leo it was a rare collector's item and when that didn't work he made Leo promise to hold it for him until he could save up some money to get it back. Leo sold the gun the next day for the ten dollars it was worth.

Charlie the Labrador was hit by a snow plow that winter but escaped with a broken leg. He limps on land, but still can keep up to Stump's stick throwing off the breakwater. They spend many hours together there in the summer while Stump waits for the launches full of tourists to return with fish to clean for a fee. The fishermen are astounded when the guides agree that they should pay the cleaning guy the quarter per fish he now asks for.

PARADISE ENDURED

"Is Grandpa rich?" The ten year old looked up from the menu and waited a response from his mother.

"I suppose he's rich, he's just not very generous." The woman looked down as if she was done, but decided more needed to be said about her father. "I mean he's got it set up so I get four thousand a month and the suite upstairs, but I can only order off the menu. Three meals a day but they have to be off the menu, what would it of hurt him to let me order something special if I wanted it."

"How much will we get each month"?

"It's just twelve hundred now, but the money goes into a trust that's invested for us and we have to be twenty one to access it for anything other than college." The girl looked across the table at her brother after answering, waiting the follow up question, like an experienced mother instead of just a slightly older sister.

"Yea but how much will that be each month?"

"It all depends on how the markets do, and on how much mom spends out of the original trust."

The boy's vision of the world was that of a child and restricted to how much will I get. The girl had developed to the adult point of view and the reality that how much she would get was affected by many things including how much other people got. The mother recognized both points of view, and the inevitability of her babies growing up to take their places at a common table.

"I'm sure he thinks the money is ok, but he is a wealthy man and could take better care of me, Dad would say he's being frugal, but he's just being cheap." Her voice was practiced, the tones turned up at the end, and even though the mature voice of an adult it had the whining quality of an accomplished ten year old.

"Grandpa says the difference between cheap and frugal is whose name is on the check." The teenage girl watched her mother for a response to the confrontational statement.

"Oh really, he wasn't talking about me when he said that was he?"

The girl realizing she might be going into an area that could turn ugly, concentrated on spinning the straw in a mad circle around the edge of her Diet Coke as she looked for a response. "I don't remember when or why I just heard him saying it."

"Well your just here for another week so let's not talk about your Grandpa; let's only talk about things that will make us happy."

They were seated at a round table in a slightly dark tiki style bar and restaurant that was nestled beneath a hotel one block off Waikiki Beach. The walls were covered with the pictures of old ships, long dead seafaring men, and the body breaking hardware they had served in life.

The waitress delivered menus and water to the middle aged couple at the table behind them, and took their order for coffee as soon as possible please. Obvious tourists, they had the dazed look of cattle recently removed from a box car, but not yet shown the ramp up into the building where the mooing ended. They thanked the girl and she moved on to the woman and two children.

"Can I take your order?"

"Your new here aren't you?"

"Yes I started yesterday."

"Where are you from?"

"California."

"See Rea I told you all the prettiest girls are from California. What part?"

"Chula Vista."

"Oh yes its, nice, there. Were from Laguna Beach, but my father has a place near Monterey. How long ago did you leave the mainland?"

"I've been here almost a year now."

"I've been here forever; at least it seems that long." The whining undercurrent of her voice shifted into a melancholic hum just short of a moan.

"I could come back if you need a little more time to decide."

"No I have the menu memorized. I'd like the Macadamia nut pancakes with crisp bacon, but I'd like a bowl of whipped cream instead of that dreadful coconut syrup."

"I'm sorry Mam but the manager told me about the arrangement your father has with the hotel, I could ask him if they can change it around a bit, but I'd have to clear it with him first."

"There's no point I know what he'd say. Bring on the syrup, what the heck." Her hands moved acknowledging defeat or acceptance, and making a little fan like pair of wings in front of her shoulders. When the waitress left with the three orders the woman turned to her daughter. "See that's what I was talking about. How humiliating, that a server would know about "our arrangement", I mean really. Your Grandfather should be ashamed causing this kind of embarrassment over a bowl of whipped cream."

"Why can't you order what you want mom?" The boy asked from nearby where he was trying to pry loose a cutting tool designed to slice blubber off dead whales, that was bolted to the faux weathered ship boards that made up the walls. The girl looked up from her soda curious about the answer her mother would give.

"He thought I spend too much of his money ordering expensive food I didn't eat when it was served. I think that's what bothered him the most, all old people talk about is "The Depression" and how hard things were "for them" like any food I left on my plate somehow is related to suffering sixty years ago. He doesn't see that people grow, that we can change. So here I am trapped, being talked about by workers in a second rate hotel."

"This place doesn't seem so bad." The boy said as he moved from the well anchored hacking instrument and on to a long shafted harpoon.

"No, but there are so many places so much nicer. Your Grandpa made sure it was just enough that if friends heard of where I was staying he wouldn't need to make up any excuses."

"Couldn't you just pay for the whipped cream out of your own money mom?"

"That isn't the point I'm making Rea. Your Grandfather is a wealthy man and he should feel ashamed of the way I'm forced to live. All it would take is a call to the manager here to make my life a little more bearable, a little less the same every boring day."

A gentle rain started to fall outside, more like mist sprayed on aging vegetables at a grocery store than a shower. Some people ran for the shelter of nearby buildings, the locals smiled and went about their business knowing it would stop as suddenly as it started, welcoming the brief cool that would follow, before the hot side walks and streets turned the rain into steam. A homeless person walked by at a fast pace talking and gesturing excitedly to himself and turned into an ABC store. Tiny doves continued their never ending delicate shuffle for crumbs in the litter under a line of palm trees across the street as dark colored myna birds screeched down at passersby from the limbs of trees in the park.

In the restaurant the pair of tourists ordered their breakfasts, and said yes to more coffee. They talked about what time it was back in Minnesota and what they would be doing if they were at work right then. The woman had her Kauai guide book open and was making a checklist of things to do later in the week. A Robert's Tour bus roared down the street on the way to Pearl Harbor, its windows lined with expectant faces and a score of digital video recorders capturing street scenes and images the camera operators were too involved in reducing to mega pixels to see.

"What should we do after we eat?"

"I think we should go to the beach, Timmy could snorkel and I could surf, that was a wicked curl yesterday and I'd like to see if I can do better on it today."

"Rea just wants to see Bradley again; she's in Love with Bradley."

"Am not!"

Rea and her brother both giggled over some secret formula of words in their exchange as Mom continued to fume over un-won battles and un-forgiven sins.

The waitress made her way through the forest of old hemp ropes and sweat stained hickory carrying a tray on her shoulder filled with crisp bacon, sausages, and stacks of golden pancakes, with one hand she pulled a folding stand from behind a timber, which could have come from a sailing ship, but now stood as a beam supporting nothing, unfolded it, and efficiently set the heaped tray of food down to an un-appreciating audience. In the middle of the tray sat a bowl filled with whipped cream.

"Chuck wasn't in the kitchen and I figured a bowl of whipped cream won't break the place."

"Thanks so much, you are an angel. Us California Girls have to stick together don't we."

The waitress walked away checking the tourist's need for caffeine and assuring them their orders would be out in just a few minutes.

"Well at least she was nice, it just shows that when your good to people their nice back." She scooped a spoon of cream from the bowl and deposited it on the top of her stack of pancakes. "I can't believe this, look Rea it isn't even real whipped cream, it's like, I don't know, Cool Whip, or some kind of whipped topping. They might as well have sent it out in the plastic container, or brought out the squirt can."

Paradise Denied
Angelica Doesn't Want You Bothering Her Anymore

The man left the ABC store his eyes downcast both to avoid contact with others and to maintain his constant search for coins lost from shopper's pockets. His arms and hands were still, clasping a paper bag covered bottle of wine in tight to his chest. Close up his relentless talk had meaning, but only occasional context with his surroundings.

"She comes in at noon, gives me plenty of time to find her something nice."

"Don't like that kid."

"No he's a smug little snot. Seemed to think it was funny me asking about her."

"She should find a better place to work! Coming down here and then needing to get home so late. Say's she's married, but what kind of man would let his wife be taking the bus that late. She needs someone who'll protect her. Maybe I should follow her home again, only not try to talk to her, not get so close this time, just take the same bus is all in case someone tries something on her."

The perceived someone's propelled his conversation into an argument and one hand left the protective embrace of his bottle and orchestrated a tongue lashing. He moved through the pedestrian traffic like Moses through the Red Sea, it opened in front and closed behind. The sidewalks were lined with a thousand shops selling T-Shirts and postcards, packets of treats boldly proclaiming the distance traveled by the buyer, mugs, brightly flowered dresses, and loud shirts with coconut shell buttons. It was early and the air still a caress that smelled of sweet flowers and diesel exhaust. He turned and walked down a palm lined avenue towards the beach. In the narrow gap between luxury hotels he could see distant waves roll as the endlessly moving water contacted the submerged sea floor.

The McDonald's looked busy enough with breakfast customers, and he badly needed to use their bathrooms. The public facilities near the ocean were locked tight until later in the morning when people with homes and hotel rooms would start to arrive for a day of recreation. The scattered street people were expected to hold it, or face scorn and potential arrests if nature made untimely demands and an exposed alley happened to be the only available privacy. He entered the McDonald's quickly and made a direct assault on the toilets.

"Sir the restrooms are for paying customers only." A quick eyed assistant manager made the statement on the move as he hurried to place himself between the man and his obvious objective.

"I'm gonna buy something after, but I gotta go now."

"Look mister you've pulled this before, none of you guys ever buy anything and we end up cleaning up messes all morning long."

"What am I supposed to do crap my pants?"

The breakfast crowd was growing uncomfortable with the argument and several started to sidle towards the exit. The others waited for the egg muffins, fried Spam, and plastic cups of fresh sliced pineapple to be brought out to the counter, trying to appear distant and unaware.

"Look you're either headed outta here in five seconds or I'm calling the cops."

The man left cussing the young man and making obscene gestures at the open stares of the people who'd made purchases and earned the right to use the toilet at their leisure. He was tempted to drop his pants in front of the plate glass windows, but knew he would end up inpatient again if he did. Instead he went behind the building and relieved himself with his back leaning against the service entrance. His vengeance would be that who ever opened it next would possibly step in his mess or at least smear it the full sweep of the large metal door.

He'd come to Hawaii while still somewhat functional, after his second psychotic break and at the end of his only marriage. A manic spiral was just beginning, he left convinced that sun and fresh fruit would heal him of Fargo, of winter, of a wife who expected so much. He'd always been able to find jobs and he did in Honolulu, several of them, but the flight of thoughts and the suspicions kept him from keeping them. Two years ago he'd gone homeless, living from dumpsters and handouts. When he was feeling sociable, which wasn't so often anymore, he would joke with some of the others about what a great place to be homeless, Waikiki Beach, guilty tourists with pockets full of change, and you could always work on your tan. A group of his peers sat on a cement bench several hundred feet down shore from where he walked out to the beach walk. The sand was nearly deserted, but would be filling up soon as it did every day. They yelled at him in a friendly manner, but he guessed they saw his bottle so he headed back to the park and the shade of the trees. A policeman on a bicycle seemed to be studying him so he turned down a different street and had to walk by the McDonalds again. He wished he hadn't defecated on their doorstep, all he needed was the junior executive to spot him. Maybe they hadn't needed to use the door yet. He rushed by the window and got the "stink eye" from the man cleaning up around the outside tables, which could mean they had discovered his deposit, or it could just be the distrust people with little had for the ones with nothing.

In the trees he slowed to a walk and peered ahead towards the thicket bordered by chain link fence for signs of others hiding out from the sun. Scattered on the grass were pieces of cardboard and carpet, the filthy remains of cheap grass mats many of the stores sold, even a few bodies of men sleeping off the effects of chemical excesses. He sat down and leaned against the trunk of a tree, looked back in the direction he'd entered the shade and opened the bottle. It wasn't until he'd cracked the top that he noticed a movement under a near by tree, a scrap of soiled khaki with a dark leg beneath peaking out no more than twenty feet from him. Who ever it was didn't seem too interested in his bottle, and in fact was apparently hiding from him. He couldn't stand having anyone that close and not know what they were up to while he drank, so he slipped backwards a few feet to better see the intruder.

"Hey Bobby ya steal that thing, or are ya turning surfer on us?"

Bobby pulled a medium sized surf board further into the shade of the Banyan tree. He was young, hardly more than a teenager, but his hair and clothing told the story of a long run at homelessness.

"Didn't steal nothing, found it washed up this morning when I was shell hunting."

"Some shark ate good last night. You ought'a take it down to the cops, maybe help em figure out where the guy ended up."

"Like that's what you'd do Danno. Me an this board are headed to Pacific Rim Pawn as soon as they open up."

Daniel, who had become Danno one drunken night after sharing with his new companions that the idea of his move to The Islands had come to him during a spell of unemployment while watching afternoon reruns of Hawaii Five O, looked at Bobby and speculated on his chances at a cut in the profits.

"Want some Cabernet?"

Bobby looked doubtfully at Daniel suspecting a trap in the offered bottle.

"You wouldn't know a Cabernet if ya was drowning in the crap."

The temptation and his superior size provided him with a decision, Bobby picked up the things he had stashed behind the tree and his ill gotten surf board and joined Daniel in his bit of shade. The mesh snorkel gear bag captured Daniels attention immediately. Bobby supplemented his SSI check by snorkeling early each morning just off the edge of the beach and selling his illegally gathered sea shells to the tourists. Nestled in the bottom of the bag in between the stubby boogey boarder swim fins lay a small but perfect conch shell. Beautifully shaped, with finger like horny protrusions spaced protectively around its soft insides, a spiral of wonderfully webbed colors, recently camouflage, now simply an ornate curse assuring it for a short time a place of prominence in someone's bathroom, but just as assuredly given time, consignment to a box in storage.

"How much ya want for that little conch?"

"It ain't that little!"

"What ya take for it?"

"I might let ya look at it for that bottle before ya wrap them diseased lips of yours around it again."

"Be a damn shame if the cops were to hear about somebody finding a surfboard, specially if it turned out it belonged to someone that went swimming an never came back."

Daniel left the copse of shrubs shortly after noon with a small but perfect conch held protectively at his side. The compromised amount of wine left him just short of inebriation. He and Bobby had passed the bottle back and forth and told lies, sharing their particular philosophies on life as the morning slipped away joining all the mornings that had gone before this one.

In a dumpster behind a lei stand Daniel searched for the freshest of yesterdays discarded flowers to add to his offering. The tour buses were running heavy as he poked through the discarded blossoms, and as they sat at the corner waiting to make the turn towards more beauty some of the cargo watched the dirty man immerse himself in the fragrant trash. A few pointed him out to one another, but the rest ignored his plight and listened to the driver tell them where they would be going next. He emerged triumphant with a handful of lavender orchids, the edges of their petals drooping slightly.

At the nearest ABC Store a pair of tourists looked through postcards, each stood by a rack, frequently holding up a card for the other to judge, occasionally the card was rejected, most were added to the stack each held in their hands. In the next aisle a dark haired woman in a brightly flowered shirt lined up bags of blended coffee on a well stocked shelf. She moved with efficiency fronting the older bags and moving the misplaced flavors to their rightful spot in the display.

"Here comes your boyfriend Angelica." A young man at the checkout counter near the front of the store looked back to make sure his co-worker had heard what he thought was a humorous warning. The mixed look of irritation and dread assured him that she had. "Didn't your momma ever tell you not to talk to strangers?' She didn't respond, so he felt the need to reinforce his tutorial on survival. "Next time maybe you'll listen to her."

"I just felt sorry for him, he seemed so alone, so I'd listen to him while I worked. How was I to know he was such a fruitcake. He even followed me home on the bus one night after work, and tried to talk to me." She looked out the window and saw the man crossing the street towards the store front. "He's really starting to creep me out. I'm going to go hide out in the back till he leaves." As she retreated to the storeroom, the man outside crossed the sidewalk and entered the store. The tourists paused in the search for manufactured memories as the tension in the room penetrated their pursuit.

"Where's Angelica? You told me she'd be here by noon."

"Why don't you leave her alone? She doesn't want you bothering her anymore."

" Bothering her, is that what she said? You're the one saying that, she'd never say something like that. Just go get her and let me talk to her. I got something for her." The man held up his beautiful shell and fading flowers as if they would sway the argument.

"Following people home after work is bothering them. Look just do yourself and her a favor and get out'a here, she doesn't want you hanging around. If you come in here again I'll call the cops and tell them you've been stalking her."

That the woman had told a co-worker, about being followed seemed to penetrate the layers of fantasy he had built up. He opened his mouth to say he didn't want anything, just to protect her, but only silent wine tainted breath came out. He could see how this kid might misjudge his intentions, but the woman should have known of his concern and love. "I'll come back, I gotta tell her I never would have hurt her, I was sent to protect her."

"If you ever bother her again I'm calling the cops, and I'll tell her she should do the same."

The man left the ABC Store knowing the few minutes he counted on each day, telling her stories, and the comments she made in that softly accented voice were over. And they would be out there waiting for her each night as it grew dark, waiting for her to leave without his protection. He looked at his hands and saw the rejected offering, it slipped from his fingers and fell to the sidewalk breaking one of the spiny protective fingers. He walked silently down the crowded street, his eyes shifting from person to person desperately seeking eye contact, hoping for a common bond, a spark acknowledging their shared humanity. Within a block he had given up and was once again visually sweeping the cement for dropped change.

Snapshots
or
Paradise Captured

The tourist couple stood behind a bus stop bench half listening as an old Asian man talked to an exhausted looking woman in a flower print housekeeping uniform from one of the nearby hotel towers. Her white jogging shoes at the ends of tired outstretched legs were unlaced and stained. She listened politely to his stories of children and grandchildren and responded to his questions about the possibility of common acquaintances, but looked down the street squinting at each approaching bus hoping for the number that would carry her away. The tourists studied their Hawaii Handbook and watched for a number 57 beach bus the book said would take them to Hanauma Bay.

"Does old Harry Kuta still work at the front desk?"

"No I don't think I've ever heard of him."

Undaunted the old man went on to tell a story about Harry. The woman sat up straighter staring down the street silently willing her bus to appear.

The tourist woman shifted her beach bag from one shoulder to the other. "How much money do we have with us?"

The man looked annoyed but dug the thin fabric wallet out of the pocket of his swim trunk shorts and opened the Velcro closure. "Eight bucks."

"Do you think that will be enough?"

"We have enough. We had more than enough before you bought the beach towel and all those postcards."

"You think it's a pretty towel don't you?" The towel in question was pulled from her mesh beach bag and held up for the hundredth time for a determination of relative worth. "And you had a thicker stack of cards than I did."

The man glanced at the bright red towel with its white hibiscus pattern, and remembered the tortured time inspecting each towel from the endless shelf of towels as they were presented to him for an opinion. "It's just fine, and all of my cards came from the five for a dollar rack."

"I think we should go get more money from the hotel safe."

"Eight bucks is all we need for the bus and you already have that lovely towel. What more could you possibly need? Besides if we take more we'll have to take turns snorkeling and watching the stuff, plus we might miss the bus."

"Ok." The one word response held more meaning than many editorials.

An arriving bus spared the weary Hotel Worker from the well intentioned ramblings of the old man. She exchanged some small talk with the driver and took a seat watching as her vacated spot on the bench was taken by a large cartoonish looking tourist woman in a brilliantly colored floral dress. The elderly woman's large nose was heavily coated in white cream, her head crowned with a straw hat ribboned in material rivaling the dress. The two occupiers of the bench struck up an immediate conversation. The Hotel Worker leaned her head back on the seat and closed her eyes as the bus roared off down the street.

"Are you sure it's the number 57 bus we need to take? I think we should ask someone, that's an old book and things might have changed."

"You can ask the driver when the bus gets here if you don't trust the book."

The woman opened the beach bag apparently to take another look at the towel, but her gaze shifted to the direction she must have thought home was. "I hope the animals are ok."

"I read somewhere that to a dog or a cat two weeks is the same as two days, because they don't have any real concept of time."

"How would anyone know what an animal's concept of time is? It sounds like something people who travel a lot would come up with so they don't feel guilty leaving their pets."

"I don't know it's just something I read, it must work cause I don't feel guilty."

"Neither do I, I was just wondering how they're doing."

"Number 57 TheBus, see I told you these things work like a clock." The man pointed down the street as a bus bearing the number 57 pulled out of traffic and headed for the curb in front of them. They joined the front of the line and walked up the steps through the hissing hydraulic doors.

"Does this bus go to Hananuma Bay?"

"No, but it goes to Hanauma Bay." The driver watched dollar bills disappear into the money taking machine. "Please take a seat."

The tourists filed down the corridor as more people boarded the already crowded bus. They found two seats together near the rear exit and sat down.

"You have to ask next time."

"If you would have just trusted the book you wouldn't have needed to ask at all. Don't be embarrassed, it's not a big deal, no one knows you here anyway, besides they're probably used to tourist butchering the names of places."

"Your so comforting it's like you always know just what to say."

The man ignored the sarcasm in his wife's voice. "Don't mention it, that's what I'm here for. What we'll do from now on is every time someone corrects us for screwing up a place's name, we'll remember how the lady at the airport pronounced Bemidji. That way we won't feel so stupid."

From the seat behind them a female voice with familiar mid-western accent interrupted them. "Did I hear you say you were from Bemidji?"

The woman turned in her seat to see who was talking to them, and saw a lady who looked to be in her mid 40s in the standard issue floral dress, this one in a coral hue. "No but that's where we flew out of yesterday, or was it the day before, this time change and being away from home has me all screwed up. We live about thirty miles from Bemidji."

"Oh, My God you just got here, I envy you so much. We only have two days left and then it's back to Des Moines. We spend a week every summer at a resort near Blackduck, so we've been in Bemidji lots of times. This year we spent our vacation money to come here so we won't be going to the cabin."

The man sitting next to her broke into the conversation. "I'd say more like the next three years for what this trip cost."

The lady from Des Moines looked unsympathetically at her husband. "Gerald doesn't much like Hawaii. He says it's like a string of jewelry stores hooked together by T-Shirt shops and sand."

"It was ok for the first couple days. I'm just tired of shopping."

"He thinks the perfect vacation is spent fishing and drinking beer on the porch by the lake. How long are you here for?"

"Just two days in Honolulu, then we go to Kauai for five days and then to Maui for five."

"See Gerald that's what we should have done. We spent all six days here, and I guess it did get a little boring, for him anyway."

"How's the food? Did you find any fun places to eat?"

"It's pretty much like we have back home. There's a nice House of Pancakes down from our Hotel, and an Applebee's, a Chili's, and lets see, oh just about anything you can find in Des Moines they have here. We went to a luau one night, it was part of the package from our tour, the pork was good, but some of the dishes were a little bit strange."

"Did you try any really great Asian restaurants? We only have two nights here so we want to go someplace really special."

"We don't care for Chinese food. Gerald was in the Navy and he says you never know what you're eating in one of those places. Mostly we just went to the beach or looked at shops, Pearl Harbor, some of the museums, our package had everything pretty much planned, but we had a couple free days and this is one of them."

The two men had turned to their windows and looked out at the passing street scene as their wives talked. They were in an area of tall hotels with shops below and between, identical to the area they had just left and to the one they were just entering. The tourists walking and the locals working all seemed dressed from the same shops, a teeming bright splash of humanity surging back and forth in a narrow corridor far below a cement and glass skyline.

TheBus turned away from blocked out Ocean and accelerated into the hectic traffic of Interstate. The driver made an announcement even the new arrivals were familiar with about the freeway not actually hooking up to any roads on the West Coast, that it was an Interstate in funding only, and then got down to the job of careening through the zigzagging cars and trucks. It could have been a highway anywhere if not for the palm trees and beautiful flowers covering most of the growing thing in sight. The neighborhoods beyond the road stacked towards nearby mountains, terraced gradients measuring time and stages of development as the land went from tropical dream to real estate nightmare. After a quick foray on Interstate the tri-colored bus took an exit and reentered the slower traffic of what had changed from narrow city thoroughfare to a two lane highway between rows of crowded together houses and apartment buildings. At side streets the passengers on the right of the bus were given brief glimpses of Ocean and the more beautiful homes of those who could afford to live several blocks away in that direction.

Gradually the neighborhoods ended as the highway wound its way back and forth between grassy hills and rock outcroppings. At the top of the more spectacular rises scenic outlook points allowed the slower traffic to pull over and admire the view. A group of people got off at a stop billed as a trailhead for hikers. Several makeshift stands with homemade signs advertising T-shirts, bottled water, and everything a person might need for a walk were set up in the parking area. The Ocean was more visible now and only disappeared when the land rose up to obstruct it. The bus slowed and made a sharp right turn off the highway and went over a set of speed bumps as it headed down hill into a large, crowded state park. Tour busses and limousines from hotels lined the area near a low rock wall and cars took up the parking spots further back. TheBus looped around the lot, pulled up to its stop, and all the doors opened.

People pulled together their beach bags and lunch boxes and shuffled off, the locals were more organized and less hurried. The tourist couple from the bus stop exited from the nearby rear door and fell in behind the group walking towards the rock wall and the Ocean beyond. They stopped in front of the sign welcoming them to Hanauma Bay State Underwater Park and telling them the rule of not feeding the fish and some other park basics.

"I never even thought about an admission fee. Whoever heard of charging someone to go swimming?"

"The book didn't say anything about this."

"Like I said it's an old book."

The couple looked over the edge of the cliff at a path crowded with people going down and coming up from the sparkling sand beach bordering the inner curve of a sea water flooded volcanic crater. The pure aqua blue waters were spotted with people snorkeling in between and over submerged coral beds. The inner walls of the volcano narrowed on the Ocean side but ended abruptly where they had collapsed into the sea giving the crater its three quarter moon shape and allowing the Pacific in. They stood on the brink and watched their recent traveling companions get in the line stretching down around the curving sides of the volcano and begin their decent. Either could have said the many words available to totally ruin the day, reminders of trips not taken back to the hotel safe or of beautiful beach towels. Instead they waited for the next bus back to Waikiki at the top of an extinct volcano. Watching people swim, sun, and eat picnics in the shade of trees bordering a beach captured in several of their recently purchased postcards.

"Smile."

The man turned as his wife clicked a picture on their disposable camera. It captured him with the Ocean and partial moon crater behind. "Do you think an underwater camera is going to work out of the water?"

"I don't know but we'll find out."

NOVEMBER

I'd just turned seventeen that fall and split my time between being sure I knew everything I needed, and occasional moments of clarity when I either feared the future, or felt just being seventeen was more than I was equipped to handle. The possibility of something happening to make either confidence or worry irrelevant seemed impossible.

The alarm clattered, and leaving my warm blankets only made sense if it meant I could somehow regain that wonderful four-thirty in the morning sleep. In November dreams had more allure than the reality of hunting ducks, especially at four-thirty.

I got all goose bumpy running around the room in the cold trying to remember where everything was.

When I had all my layers of clothes pulled on I reached over and clicked off the light. I shut the bedroom door and softly walked down stairs. I must have been about half-way down when I heard the door to Dad and Mom's room open up.

"Where you going this morning Henry?" Dad whispered in the darkness.

"Stony, maybe Middle Point, depends on what the weathers doing."

"Be careful of that wind, it's Northwest and coming all the way across the lake."

"Sure thing Dad."

I don't know why he had to say that. It's like he doesn't think I know enough to set up on a sheltered point. Up above I could hear his bed spring squeak as he sat back down. Then I heard Mom say something. I couldn't quite catch what it was, but Dad said yes to what ever she'd said.

I picked up my shot gun and hunting coat and then stepped outside. Its cold, I have to put my gun down and pull my hunting coat on. My breath comes out in clouds and disappears into the starless sky. I check the boat, stuck slant-wise in the back of the pick up and tied down real good. The decoy sacks are tucked up under where they can't bounce out.

"Morning Henry ya look so pretty in the morning." Steve emerged from the dark down by the street.

He was the most cheerful person I ever met at that time of the day. I guess some people are just like that.

"Is Danny here yet?"

"Na, he must still be sleeping, his lights were off when I walked by his place."

"He's always holding things up. "You got any gum?"

Steve reached into his shell pocket and came out with a pack of Wrigley's Spearmint. It was all dirty with dried on blood and duck feathers. I looked at the stick he handed me all crumpled up and funny, so old it was brittle. I picked off the foil and stuck it in my mouth. I don't know what they put in that stuff, but after sitting in his jacket for all that time it still tasted like mint.

When we got to Danny's there was a light on up in his room so I pulled up to the curb and shut off the truck. Steve reached over and honked the horn to make sure

Danny knew we were there.

"That ought to make his ma mad."

Just then their front door opened and out came Danny, his boots untied, holding his coat and gun. He seemed to be in a hurry. His mom was right behind him, in one of those old quilted house coats.

"Daniel, are you sure you don't need a scarf?"

"Please! Be quiet ma, just let me alone. I got everything I need, go back to bed."

"Well, don't get wet, you know you're just getting over a cold, and the flu season is here now too."

Danny was to the door of the truck and sliding his shotgun in when she finally went back in the house. He sat down kind of upset and didn't say anything. The first mile or so out of town was real quiet. Then Steve looked over at me and said, "Now Henry, did you bring your scarf and mittens. You know it's the tuberculosis season."

We both laughed for about another two miles. Danny didn't seem to think it was all that humorous, he just glared out the window and said, "Smart asses."

Once the heater got blowing warm air, it quieted down. When we got to the lake I backed down to the edge of the little harbor on the edge of the point. With a Northwest wind the sheltered side of Stony Point was the only safe place so we set up there.

Outside it was freezing. The wind cut through my coat, and snow was falling. Flakes stung as they hit my cheeks and glowed in the truck's headlights. Above we heard the whistle of wings cutting through the darkness. You could feel it was going to be a perfect day.

Danny rowed the boat out to the end of the point and I sat in the back with the decoy sacks. We could see the flashlight bobbing up and down as Steve walked along the shore, climbing over rocks and screwing around. Steve was supposed to hold the light on us and tell us if we were out too far. In the blackness we couldn't see where shore was and we didn't want to set decoys too far out or too close to where we were going to hide.

All of a sudden Steve started flashing the light off and on like Morris Code or something.

"What are you doing in there?"

"I'll flash twice if you're in the right spot and three times if you're out too far."

"Bullshit! We can hear you, just tell us and keep the light on."

I started pulling decoys out and unwinding the cords. Sometimes one would come out untangled but it seemed that most of them had their weights tangled up with another. No matter how careful you are wrapping them up, when it's cold and early the things are tangled. After what seemed an hour, I had a bag and a half out and of my fingers just wouldn't cooperate any more.

"That's enough, the way their flying we don't even need that many."

It was more than just an excuse to stop setting decoys; the whole time we'd been out there I could hear ducks going over. Danny rowed into shore while I tucked my hands up inside my coat and into my armpits; they felt like ice at first, by the time we got to the harbor I could feel enough to pull the trigger on my shotgun, but nothing more intricate than that.

It was surprising; Steve was standing there with the flashlight. Usually he'd hide out on the end of the point or where ever the blind was and we'd have to stumble through the dark trying to find him. This morning he was waiting to catch the boat and help pull it up and into cover. Danny and I drove the pick up back into the woods so it wouldn't flare the ducks, and grabbed our guns to head down the point.

"You know what he's going a do don't ya? He'll get down to the blind and shut the flashlight off. I don't know why ya let him have the flashlight."

"Can you imagine the crap he'd pull out in the boat? If he rowed he'd be splashing me with the oars, if he was setting decoys he'd screw around with his Donald Duck voice to be funny. This time he wasn't so damn tricky." I reached under the seat and pulled out a silver Ray-O-Vac, switched it on, and walked down the beach towards the blind.

On Stony there isn't really much of a blind. The point is solid rock and not much grows there. The only way to hide from the ducks is to find a rock that's lower than the rest and sit on it. The other rocks break your silhouette if you stay crouched down just a little bit.

Out on the end of the point we heard a single shotgun blast and then Steve started yelling, "I got that one!"

He's so full of crap, without the flashlight a person couldn't see his hand a foot in front of his face. When we got out to the blind he was sitting on a rock, eating an apple, as if nothing had happened.

"You guys so afraid of the dark that ya bring two flashlights?"

"Na, we just know you so well that we prepare ourselves before we even let ya in the truck."

Steve had picked a spot about in the middle of the point, with decoys on each side of him. This spot wasn't the best for hunting unless the birds came from the front. Danny or I, on the ends, would get the first shots, but from the middle he must have figured he could pester and amuse us equally.

I picked a rock about six feet down shore from Steve. It had a bigger rock behind so I could lean on it and rest my back. Sometime during night the wind had switched, because the rocks were covered with a layer of ice. Using a smaller rock I broke what I could off my boulder before I sat down.

This was the time of the morning when I always started wondering about things. Like why did I leave those nice warm sheets and quilts to come out here and sit on an icy rock? I could remember how good they felt and how nice it would have been just to have rolled over and snuggled down in for about three more hours. My family was probably still sleeping, here I sit, trying to make as little a target as I could for the wet snow that was blowing in from behind on the November wind.

Danny walked over and squatted down between us.

"You guys got any extra shells, Ma must of washed my hunting coat."

"Who cleans uh hunting coat anyway? My Ma ever did something like that I'd leave home."

I dug into my shell pockets and took out three from each side. Danny thanked me and embraced Steve like a Frenchmen would when he handed over nine shells. That was one thing good about my Ma; she'd never go around trying to take the luck out of the guy's hunting jacket by washing it.

The first bunch of ducks broke the decoys from down on Danny's side. It was so dark that we heard them way before we saw anything. There were four Goldeneyes. In the darkness they were black and white blotches, twisting and turning as they swung around belly up to the decoys. Two died before they hit the water, one landed and then came up out beyond the decoys flying when it surfaced. The hen was swimming down shore, Danny cripple shot her.

"That was great huh? I made a beautiful shot on that drake. He just folded up pretty as could be." Steve always talked like that; soon he'd be claiming he shot all three.

"Since you made such a pretty shot on it, you'd probably be the best one to row out and get them." Steve just grinned and headed for the boat.

A pair of blue bills came over the end of the point and then flared off when they saw the boat.

"Hurry up Steve, your screwing us up." He stopped trying to pick up the last duck with the end of the oar and reached over the edge and grabbed it. He was almost into shore when a single bill came in from Danny's side. Danny dropped it with one shot.

"Oh, say old boy, would you fetch that bird for me? There's a good chap, splendid, retrieve it like a good fellow." Steve made an obscene gesture but the rules were the rules so he rowed back out for the duck.

When Steve got back to the blind he threw the blue bill at Danny.

"There ya go Daniel," he sounded so much like Danny's mom I had to laugh. "Ducks down towards Bear Island."

Steve pointed, there must have been two or three hundred of them. Moving like a smudge on the horizon through the snow spotted sky. All three of us tried to sink lower down into our rocks. Then I started to think, "I'll bet that damn Steve screws us up." I glared down at him, but he was scrunched down with just his eyes moving as he looked from one end of the flock to the other. I slowly turned my head back towards the flock. In a few minutes they'd be in range, then a splinter group flared off suddenly and took them all back down the point.

About 8:30 I heard Danny gasp so I looked down his way. Out beyond the point, over rough water, there were about forty swans, flying so low that their wing tips seemed to bounce up out of the waves as they flew. The snow was swarming around them; their bodies arching and dipping like snakes. The necks stuck out in front about two feet and gave them even more movement. As quick as they showed up they were gone, disappearing into the snow that was getting heavier as the morning went by. Seeing that made me feel better about the raft of ducks we almost had.

It wasn't too long after the swans had gone by when we had another bunch of whistlers come screaming over the point from behind us. They were so low that their wings, sounded like a jets. They hit the end of the decoys before we could even get the safeties off on our guns. Just when I figured we were screwed again, they turned, like a precision flying team, winged in this tight little half-circle and bellied up to our set. There were eight of them, all drakes, the white patches on their cheeks looked like great big blank eyes staring out at you. We knocked down six, five were good hits, either laying dead on the water or just barely moving. The sixth one kept diving and heading down shore with Steve after him. The duck stayed within range, but every time he'd surface Steve would be running, and every time Steve got his gun up, the duck would dive. He kept this up for about a half a mile. Then all of a sudden he went down and never came back up. My dad told me once that when they do that their down on bottom, holding onto weeds or something.

We'd hit that slow period about 10:00 when it seems that picking up the decoys and going home wouldn't be at all that bad of an idea. Steve was throwing little pebbles at us and then looking out at the decoys like he was seriously watching for ducks. He'd look real hurt when you told him to knock it off. I was about to start tossing back at him when I saw a pair of Buffleheads. They were close to shore so Danny and Steve couldn't see them, I decided to be quiet and give Steve a scare. I nonchalantly half turned my back. He hit me in the back with a couple of pebbles, but I didn't even look back at him. I clicked the safety off when the ducks were about a hundred yards out, and didn't let on that there was anything in the air except Steve's annoying stones. I shot the lead one just as it crossed over the decoys, behind me I could hear Steve yell, "What the hell are you shooting at?" I was off with my second shot, but the third one dropped him, just not very well. He didn't dive or anything, just started swimming towards Bear Island, his little wing flip-flopping in the water behind him as he swam out towards deeper water.

I ran down shore as fast as I could, stumbling over rocks and trying to protect my gun, pushed the boat out, and jumped in. It was a small boat, and a little unsteady to be jumping around in very much, but I was confident. With the gun across my lap I began rowing. The Bufflehead was out about two hundred yards swimming slowly towards the rough water. I stopped to slip in three shells and started rowing again. He kept a little ahead of me no matter how hard I rowed. I gained, but it never seemed quite enough to bring him into range. The water was getting choppy and the snow was coming down hard enough that shore was gray and blurry. I felt like I should probably turn around and forget about it. Beyond the shelter of the point the waves were getting bigger. I looked over my shoulder, the duck was close, just a little further and he'd be in range. Besides going down wind like this wasn't bad. "Yeah, but what about when ya have to turn around. I've turned it around in heavier waves than this, Yeah in the summer, this isn't July." It wasn't either. This was that cold dark November water like a gun barrel. The snow made it seem even more threatening. I looked at the duck; in about fifty more yards I'd have him. "Look your out this far, they'll really think you're a pussy if you turn back now, just go for it." It would be all over school that I chickened out if I quit now. I rowed even further. The waves were so large now that my oars would skip off the tops sometimes and I wouldn't gain anything. The snow was smothering me. Every breath an effort, no matter how many I took I couldn't get any air. My heart was pounding so hard that my rib cage was about to burst. I looked over my shoulder and he was real close. I dropped the oars, grabbed my gun, spun around, and kind of half-kneeled, half-crouched on the plank seat. I waited until he topped the crest of a wave and I had a clear shot. He was looking back at me when I shot, looking right down into me and seeing all my fear of death just as he faced his. He died quickly in a puff of smoke and a spray of lead. I could almost feel mine coming. Icy water smothering me, even more than the falling snow smothered me, and the weight of my soaked clothes drawing me down into that dark water. I put the gun down and rowed for the duck. I picked him up as we both crested a wave. He wasn't much bigger than my hand. His little cheek spot made him almost toy like.

I timed my turn on the next crest, dragging back with all my strength on the right oar. The little boat responded just like it did in the summer and spun in a quick turn.

It was the next wave that came in over the side, just the top of it, but enough to drench me. I kept rowing. I had to have speed or I'd get caught by another crest, speed to make my turn for shore. The next stroke on my right side skipped off a wave top not catching anything. More water was coming over the edge. It slowed me. Everything was so damn slow. The decoy sack was bumping against my leg now, floating back and forth with the wash of waves inside the boat. This had to be it. If I couldn't turn at the speed I had, I just wouldn't turn. I pulled back on the left oar just as the boat rode over the next wave and drove hard with the right. It turned, slow, but enough. Enough to get my bow cutting into the waves like it was supposed to. I felt I could make it now my broadside wasn't catching the wind. I heard yelling behind me in the snow. From now on each stroke has to catch the same amount of water. If one skips off the top and the other digs in I'll be sideways again. A Bluebill decoy floating out of the sack rapped its plastic bill against the side of the boat. I looked down and saw water up to my calves. With each wave water would slop in over the trough where the motor should be. I kept rowing. It seemed now that with each pull the waves were getting smaller and it took less effort to keep the boat headed for shore. It was safe now to look over my shoulder and see where I was headed. I was going in about a hundred yards south of the harbor entrance, I'd been so turned around I could have been going anywhere, as long as the waves kept getting smaller I wouldn't of cared. I rowed almost to shore before I turned and headed for the harbor.

Steve and Danny were standing there waiting and caught the boat. I sloshed up to the front. My legs were so shaky I had to hold on to the gunnels for support.

"That took guts Henry; I don't care what anyone says you got guts. When you turned you were actually out of sight man, you disappeared under a wave. We were really scared; all we could do was stand here and wait. The snow was so thick we couldn't see nothing. Then Danny saw you make the turn, we yelled so loud they must a heard us in Brainerd."

Danny was standing there, not saying anything, but looking at me kind of funny. I was crying a little bit, I guess they saw because they turned around and pulled the boat up on shore to empty out the water. I sat down on a rock and started shaking. I turned around so they couldn't see, but I knew they knew. All of a sudden I had to puke but I couldn't. All I could do was gag and it hurt my throat. I could hear them go back out after the decoys and the other duck. I sat there on that rock trying to calm down. I put my hands up inside my coat and started to rock back and forth. I squeezed myself and felt better. I sat there with my teeth chattering from the cold and my feet on the beach loving the stability of solid ground. I don't know how long I sat there but all of a sudden I heard the squeak of an oar, I turned around as they reached shore.

"Danny figured you did this just so ya wouldn't have to wrap up decoys."

"You had us worried for a second there Henry, how would we a got home with you floating around out there with the truck keys in your pocket, but then Steve figured he could hot wire it."

I still couldn't talk but their joking made me feel better. I walked back into the woods and brought the truck up to the harbor. Later as we drove home and the heater got blowing good warm air it was dead quiet with each of us isolated in our thoughts. I think that was the first thing I ever learned and knew right then what I'd learned. I'd been a coward and had gotten lucky. If you're more afraid of what people might think or say, than you are of doing something really stupid, you're not being brave, no matter how dangerous it is.

MAGIC WANDS

"A long time ago people needed wild rice to make it through the winter."

The boy nodded his head as if he fully understood what his father meant. He was excited and nervous, fearful that he wouldn't be able to meet his father's expectations, knowing his family still depended on the late summer harvest to carry them through the winter. Today would be the first time he helped gather the precious grains. He would squat in front of him on the floor of the canoe and use a short stick to pull the stalks of rice over the sides of the boat and then strike the rice heads with another stick. The sticks, about the length of his skinny arms, were tapered and smooth. His father would stand behind him and push the canoe through the rice bed with a long forked pole. The forked end was made to go down through the murky water to find something to push against on the muddy fertile bottom where the rice plants took root.

"Was mom a good ricer?"

"You bet she is."

The boy looked into the cattails that lined the river his father guided them down. They towered above the boy who was finding his spot on the floor of the canoe uncomfortable. The plants rustled constantly as the canoe passed, as if unseen creatures were peering out at them from the lush cover, watching this curious pair slide so silently by.

As they neared the rice bed, the river slowed down, and spread out, creating a dozen different channels where before there had only been one. The bottom of the river turned soft, and his father's work became more difficult, he grunted slightly from the effort of moving the canoe into the thick green floating mass.

The boy picked up his two sticks, and as his mother had shown him, reached to his right for some stalks of rice near the edge of the canoe, and forced them to lean over the edge of the small boat. With the other stick he hit the bearded heads of the tall grasses with a solid blow. Many of the grains fell off and rattled into the bottom of the canoe. He hit the rice once more and then used his left hand and stick to pull rice in from that side of the boat. He thrashed that rice with his right stick and was rewarded once again with the satisfying rattle of rice striking the insides and bottom of their narrow craft.

He looked over his shoulder and said somewhat smugly, "Nothing to it."

His father smiled and chuckled knowingly and replied, "OK! Glad to hear that. Let's get busy and fill this canoe up."

They moved slowly through the bed. His father careful to not upset the boat with his inexperienced partner in it, and taking the time to let the boy get used to the job of getting the rice from each side of the canoe. The morning sun was lifting the swirls of fog that had clung to the rice bed in curling clouds that pointed up towards the sky. A few of the maples that lined the far shore blazed out in fiery reds, oranges, and yellow, clouds of black birds feeding on the rice ahead of them flew away in a roar of wings, and played the winds until settling on a different part of the bed. In the distance geese could be heard honking with a noise that sounded like packs of dogs barking.

They too were filling up on the delicious kernels of rice.

The boy heard the geese and blackbirds, but could see only rice, unending thick walls of green. Walls that stopped the slight breeze and only shifted slightly outward from the pointed nose of the canoe. His father had to warn him about beating too hard and breaking off too many stalks. He stopped briefly to pick out the stems and blades and drop them over the edge. The boy already had a slight swelling tenderness on his palms and both little fingers. They pushed on and he beat now more steadily, learning that a slightly slanting blow to the rice heads caused less litter and more grains to fall. He developed a rhythm which he felt was very good. Unknown to him, his father watched him with slight impatience thinking of his wife, and how smoothly she struck the rice, leaving so little clinging to the stalks they passed through. About how effortlessly she worked, and of how seldom she rocked the canoe by shifting her weight in search of the nonexistent comfortable position to kneel. His son's each move threatened to send them into the cold, mucky water.

The boy now realized that the whole world was this rice bed. The heat became stifling each beard of rice that touched his skin itched, and that the rice he was harvesting was alive with bugs, hopping tinny bugs, crawling lady bugs, and millions of inching ugly green worm-like caterpillars that crawled on unabated by his brushing them off. The only thing that stopped them was to squash them and they were soon replaced by another equally intrusive one. They crawled up his pants legs, under his shirt, and wherever they passed across his sweating skin it tickled and itched. This added to the twisting aching discomfort and made his father concentrate most of his efforts on steadying the canoe so that the boy's lurching from one position to another in his efforts to crush the rice worms didn't flip the canoe.

The boy looked at the floor of the boat and understood what his mother had meant by the bear rug he would gather today. Each of the ripe heavy grains of rice had a single thin beard. The heavy grains fell into the mat of rice on the floor of the canoe and because of their weight, the beard pointed towards the sky. The overall effect of thousands of hair like bristles sticking up indeed did look like his grandfather's old bear rug, only it was greenish gray, and invaded by bugs. He wished, not for the last time, that he was at his grandmothers as in years before, waiting for his parents to come home with a canoe full of rice, and that he could be there now playing with his friends. Along with this wish there evolved a prayer that he could have a magic wand that could be pointed at the endless mass of green, rice from all over the lake would come to him in swarms like bees, falling to the floor of the canoe filling it up to the point of sinking from the weight. He was very tired and bored by these labors, so he wished all the harder for this miracle to occur. But it didn't, and the day wore on. He saw a blackbird hanging sideways from a rice stalk and whispered to the bird, "Bring me your rice and have all your friends do the same," but the blackbird only jumped up ahead of the canoe and flew off to feed somewhere less crowded. To his left he could see a small opening in the rice with a mound of muddy rice stalks piled up. On the mound sat a sleek brown muskrat. "Bring me all your rice, or tell me how to make it fall here." The rodent gave him a beady-eyed stare and slipped silently into the water.

Throughout his day the boy would visualize the merciful flight of rice to their boat, and the happy sudden end to his labor. But his hands got sorer, his feet fell asleep, a rice beard went down his throat during one of his many questions to his father, and worked its way deeper itching and gagging him as it went down. The rice worms and lady bugs didn't even bother him anymore. He was a machine that thrashed on in sequence with his father's relentless poling of the canoe. And then his father said, "It's quitting time."

The boy looked down at the full canoe and realized his wish had been granted. Like magic wands the sticks and his father's poling made it possible for rice to fall layer upon layer on the floor of their boat. The magic of will had brought in this harvest. He felt proud and was thankful.

THE END